MAKE MY WISH
COME TRUE

A CHRISTMAS NOVELLA

CAROLINE LINDEN

MAKE MY WISH
COME TRUE

CHAPTER 1

DECEMBER 1813

Guinevere Barrett had kept her good humor through
getting the sack from her employer, being cheated of
her wages, having to walk into town carrying her valise, getting
slapped on the bottom by a drunk, and even being squeezed
into the dampest corner of the stagecoach with Reginald
squalling loudly in his basket on her lap for the entire journey.
What broke her was the discovery that, due to the snow flur-
rying down around them, her stagecoach had been delayed
and she had missed the last coach toward Blackthorpe
that day.

She burst into tears.

The innkeeper's wife, seeing this, hustled over with a
handkerchief. "There, dear," she consoled, tugging Gwen
away from the door as it opened to admit another traveler.
"What did you say to her, Ned?"

"Only the truth," her husband protested. "The coach
toward Blackthorpe left an hour ago, and the next one's not

until tomorrow afternoon." He turned away, already done with her. "Aye, sir? Wanting a new team, yes?"

"Oh, my," said the woman with a sympathetic glance. "Rotten luck, that."

Gwen nodded, blotting her eyes dry. "Like the rest of my luck this year." She folded the handkerchief and held it out, done with pointless tears. "Thank you, ma'am. Is there a place I could stay, until the next coach?"

She asked hesitantly, conscious of how light her purse was. She hadn't anticipated this journey, and so hadn't saved as she might have done. She also hadn't counted on her employer sacking her on the spot for requesting a fortnight's absence, but in all truth she wasn't terribly shocked when Sir Edmund followed that up by saying that he didn't care to pay her wages due, either, not when she was deserting her post on short notice.

But her gran was ill—very ill—and she was the only relation Gwen had left in this world. Gwen could accept finding another post, even without the reference Sir Edmund and Lady Branford might have provided, but if something happened to Gran, and Gwen wasn't even there to hold her hand... that, Gwen could not bear.

The innkeeper pursed her lips. Her gaze flashed over Gwen's clothing and face, no doubt leaping to very accurate conclusions. "There's a pallet in the kitchen," she said reluctantly. "It's the scullery girl's bed, but tomorrow's her day free, and she'll go home tonight. It's none too private but I could let you have it for two shillings."

Two shillings, plus meals. Gwen tried to hide her dismay and nodded. "Thank you, ma'am." The basket in her arms lurched, and she clutched it closer.

The landlady frowned. "Is that an animal in there?"

"My cat," said Gwen. "I'll take him outside," she added quickly at the woman's expression.

"Best do," said the woman. "I can't have a cat running around. Will you be wanting something to eat? Cup of tea?"

Not if she had to pay two shillings to sleep tonight, plus supper and breakfast in the morning. "Thank you, no," she said politely. "I'll just take a turn outside for some fresh air."

The landlady nodded as she bustled off. Gwen walked back outside toward the stables and released Reginald from his basket. The orange tabby cat leapt out and stretched so hard, his legs trembled. He gave her a disgruntled look before coming to wind around her ankles.

"I'm sorry," she told him. "You'll have to fend for yourself now. There's a stable right there, no doubt full of plump, tasty mice."

He sat and looked at her expectantly. He was accustomed to her sneaking out after meals with some morsels saved from her own plate. She sighed as she crouched down to scratch his neck. "I can't afford dinner," she whispered. "Until we reach Gran's, you must pretend you are a fearsome tiger, stalking your prey."

Reginald stretched up, rubbing against her hand. Gwen smiled in spite of her situation. "Just don't run off and forget me."

It was too cold to linger outside, so she turned back toward the inn. A pair of traveling chaises had recently pulled in and the horses were being unhitched, the postillions blowing on their hands and heading for the taproom. She eyed those private carriages with envy. That was how the Bradfords traveled. They'd usually left their five children at home in Gwen's care, but she'd seen their chariot when they went off to Bath or London. It was vastly more comfortable than the public stagecoach, that was certain.

As she slipped back into the warmth of the bustling taproom, it occurred to her that the Bradfords would suffer for dismissing her. They had planned to go to Bath after

Epiphany, and now they had no governess to mind their children. Gwen had promised to return from Gran's before then, but Sir Edmund had lost his temper and told her not to come back at all, if she left. Since she'd gone straight to her room and packed, she hadn't been privy to Lady Bradford's reaction to the news, but she could imagine it. Gwen wasn't precisely gloating, but it did give her some satisfaction to think that dismissing her would rebound unpleasantly upon Sir Edmund.

Everyone was crowded near the fireplace on such a cold day. Gwen found a seat in the corner behind the door, where the icy wind caused the diamond-shaped panes of the window above her head to vibrate with a soft hum. She tucked her cloak around her, settled her valise under her feet, and rested her head against the wall beside her, suddenly very tired. It had been a long day already, even though it was barely past noon. The room smelled of chicken soup and yeasty bread and ale, making her stomach rumble wistfully. Perhaps if she slept upright in this chair, she could spend some of her dwindling funds on dinner...

The landlady whisked past, setting down a tray with a steaming cup of tea in front of her. Gwen raised her head in surprise. "Oh, I didn't—"

"The gentleman over there bade me bring it," said the woman as she collected empty cups and mugs from the neighboring table. She was gone with her tray before Gwen could ask any question.

She leaned forward and peered in the direction the woman had indicated. There was a crowd over that way, just to the left of the roaring fire, but it must be the man eating alone. At least, he was the only person who seemed to sense her stare, and looked up. She raised the cup and mouthed *thank you*. He gave a fleeting smile and nodded politely before turning back to his meal.

Gwen drank the tea. It was strong and hot, and she inhaled the steam rising from it, relishing the heat on her cheeks. Lady Bradford would scold her for accepting it from a strange man— Gwen stopped herself with a smile. It no longer mattered what Lady Bradford thought. *There* was the ray of sunshine she'd been seeking.

It only grew brighter when the landlady returned with a bowl of soup. "Also from the gent," she said as she set it down on the table.

Gwen turned, open-mouthed, toward the gentleman. This time he wasn't looking at her; he seemed to be reading a letter, his dark head bent over the papers in his hand.

I think I'm in love, she thought, unable to stop herself from scooping a bite into her mouth with clumsy haste. It was hot and delicious, even if it needed salt and contained more onions than chicken. She all but licked the bowl when it was gone.

When the man by the fireplace rose from his table, she was ready. As he made his way through the room, she saw he wore a scarlet army coat under the brown scarf slung around his neck. He paid his bill and headed for the door, which was where Gwen intercepted him.

"Please, sir, I must thank you," she said, putting out a hand to stay him as he took a long cloak from a hook on the wall and swung it around his shoulders. "The landlady says you sent me the tea and soup, and I cannot tell you how much that kindness means to me."

He gave a little half-smile. He was a handsome man, though tired and dirty. Up close she could see the dust in every fold of his coat, and the growth of a day's beard on his jaw. Long dark hair fell across his forehead above warm brown eyes. "It was my pleasure, miss," he said. "You seemed upset when I arrived."

Gwen flushed. He must be the man who'd come in as she

was sobbing into the landlady's handkerchief. "A disappointment," she acknowledged. "I'm over it now."

His gaze turned piercing. "You're going to Blackthorpe."

Now she blinked and curled her hands in the folds of her pelisse. "Yes. But I arrived too late to catch the stage."

He nodded. "That coach often leaves early. I've missed it a few times myself."

"Oh?" She looked at him, then quickly away. "If only I'd known that," she said, striving for lightness. "Not that it would have helped, but I wouldn't have gone to pieces if I'd had warning it might happen."

"To pieces!" He smiled quizzically. "Missing a coach and being marooned here overnight warrants some outrage and dismay. I hope your journey isn't desperately urgent."

She bit her lip. "I'm going to see my grandmother. A day's delay is inconvenient, but..." She mustered another smile. "But you very graciously ameliorated that inconvenience. Thank you again, sir. I wish you safe travels."

He bowed. "I wish you the same, ma'am." He waited until she stepped back, then put on his hat, touched the brim briefly at her, and strode out the door.

Gwen retreated to her seat in the corner. It was more comfortable now that she wasn't hungry, and she felt a warm glow inside from both the tea and the man's kindness. He must have arrived in one of the traveling chariots she'd seen outside, since he hadn't been on the coach with her. It was so unexpected that such a man would notice a poor governess sitting alone in the corner, let alone pay for her dinner. But Gran always believed in such people; ordinary heroes, she called them, doing a small kindness that was little to them but enormous to the recipient.

She sighed, clasping her arms around Reginald's empty basket. Now she wasn't hungry, but it would be a long day and night, waiting for the coach. She'd packed in such haste, she'd not had time to retrieve all her books from the Bradford schoolroom; she had her two favorite novels in her valise, but didn't feel like re-reading either right now. She doubted there were any others to read here. Perhaps someone would discard a newspaper.

The door opened again, sending a swirl of cold air around her ankles. Gwen flinched, then started upright.

It was the kind gentleman—an officer, she realized, spotting the gold braid under his cloak as he stopped in front of her.

"I am also going in the direction of Blackthorpe," he said abruptly. "I have room in my chariot. Would you like to come with me?"

CHAPTER 2

Adrian Fitzhugh could not believe he was doing this.

She'd been sobbing her heart out when he stepped into the inn, and that must have aroused some spark of protectiveness, or even pity, in him.

Or madness.

She was a complete stranger to him, despite naming the same village that was his own destination. Her clothes were respectable but plain, and he'd heard the hesitation in her voice as she inquired about a room. He'd also heard her refuse a meal, though with a thread of longing that snagged in his mind like a burr in his collar.

But buying a meal for a penniless young woman was one thing. Offering to take her home was another.

All right, she was a very attractive young woman. It wasn't as though he hadn't noticed that, as he'd covertly watched her from across the room. Large hazel eyes, shiny curls the color of honey. She'd chosen a quiet corner of the room as her own, a rather chilly spot near the door, rather than trying to press in near the fire as most people had done, and she'd looked so woebegone.

But his travel chaise was not large, he was desperately tired, and he had to reach Blackthorpe as soon as possible. Why on earth was he doing this?

She stared up at him with those wide hazel eyes, her pink lips parted in surprise. *See*, he chastised himself, *even she thinks you're mad.* If she had any sense, she'd say no, of course she wasn't going to get into a stranger's carriage and let him carry her off...

"Oh, sir, that is... ex-exceedingly generous," she stammered. "I couldn't possibly..."

Nod and walk away, he told himself. "I am also flying home to see my grandfather," he heard himself say instead. "He is ill, like your grandmother. I couldn't abide being forced to delay an entire day."

Slowly she closed her mouth. She studied him, then nodded once. "Yes, please."

Adrian's heart leapt even as he told himself he was ten kinds of fool. He stooped to collect her worn valise.

"Oh—Oh dear." She was on her feet now, clutching a large basket, but hesitating anxiously. "I have a cat," she blurted. "I can't leave him..."

Not a cat. Cats made him sneeze. He looked into her hopeful but worried face and said, "Collect him quickly. The horses are waiting."

The smile that blazed across her face landed like a blow to his chest, and she whirled around him and out the door without another word. He caught the flash of trim ankles as she hiked up her skirts to run. The landlady saw, and she gave Adrian a narrow-eyed look. He touched his hat to her, and pulled the door closed behind him.

It was several miles still to Blackthorpe. He surveyed the sky as he walked back to the chariot, his boots crunching on the thin layer of snow that had fallen since he arrived. In fine weather, he'd expect to be home by dinner. Today, he wasn't so sure.

He put the valise into the carriage boot. "A moment," he told the postilion who stood, hands tucked under his elbows, next to the horses' heads.

"Can't wait long in this cold," the fellow warned.

Adrian looked around and finally caught sight of the young woman, down on her hands and knees in front of the stable. She seemed to be pleading, and finally a large orange cat strolled out and jumped into her basket. Adrian tore his gaze away from her nicely-shaped bottom. She was still fumbling with the straps on the basket when she hurried up beside him.

"I'm ready," she said breathlessly. The cold had brought spots of pink into her cheeks and her eyes were bright with eagerness.

"Very good," he told her, and handed her up into the char-iot, trying not to allow his hand to linger on her back. He nodded to the postilion, already in the saddle, and climbed in. He was still pulling the door closed as the horses set off, shaking their heads and snorting against the cold.

GWEN COULD NOT BELIEVE she was doing this.

She'd just got into a carriage with a strange man and set off, alone with him, bound for who-knew-where. She'd only his word that he was going to Blackthorpe; she hadn't even thought to ask the postilion where they were headed. Not that the postilion could be considered a truly objective or even benign presence, as he was being paid by the stranger.

But she'd hardly have been better off refusing, left to spend the night alone in an unfamiliar inn, possibly sleeping in the public taproom. In the morning, she would still have little money and no companion, and she'd learned that a public coach was no protection against being groped, leered at, and generally harassed.

She glanced sideways at her companion. The chaise wasn't large, but he was keeping to his side of the carriage as much as possible. He was currently wrestling with a thickly folded blanket, and having an awkward time of it, in the cramped quarters.

"Thank you, sir," she said. "I probably ought not to have accepted, but... I *am* desperate to get back to Gran." She cocked her head. "How did you know she was ill?"

He was frowning fiercely at the blanket. "You were weeping," he said absently. "At the delay. I guessed it must be an urgent reason spurring you to make a long journey at this time of year, in this weather, and that seemed a likely one." He put his arms straight out and gave a mighty shake, and the blanket finally fell in loose folds. He cleared his throat, then gingerly moved it toward her. "Here," he told her. "The hot bricks will be cold before long."

Oh yes; she hadn't even noticed the hot bricks under her feet. Feeling even more kindly disposed toward him, she tucked the blanket around herself, realizing then that it was the only one. "Oh no," she said in alarm. "You'll be cold."

He wrapped his long gray cloak around himself. "Nonsense. After sleeping in a tent in the mountains of Spain, this is remarkably cozy."

"Oh." She hesitated. "I don't even know your name. I am Guinevere Barrett."

He gave her that fleeting little smile again. "A pleasure to make your acquaintance, Miss Barrett. Captain Fitzhugh, at your service."

She blushed as he caught her fingers and gave them a brief press.

"Barrett." His eyes stayed on her face. They were a deep

dark brown, like coffee, and his gaze felt warm. "I don't know that name. Has your family been long in Blackthorpe?"

She blew out a breath. "No. It's only my grandmother who lives there, with her sister at Larkspur Cottage. I've never been."

His brow quirked. "I thought you must be very close to her..."

"Oh, I am," she assured him. "She raised me from the time I was twelve. My mother died, and my father... well, he was not prepared or able to manage a growing girl. So he left me with Gran in Norwich." She paused, reminding herself he was a stranger and surely had no interest in her life, but somehow she found herself telling him anyway. "It was best for us all. My grandfather had died the year before, and I think I must have distracted Gran from missing him, though not always for admirable reasons!" She grimaced and gave a rueful little laugh as she admitted it.

Her companion nodded. "It's a difficult age, even without losing a parent—let alone both of them."

Gwen's throat tightened for a moment. Yes, she'd lost her father, too, to the bottomless bottle of gin he'd fallen into after Mama's death. She didn't want to think about that now. "I haven't been able to visit Gran often in the last few years. She didn't like to be alone, after I was grown, so she went to live with her sister in Blackthorpe."

"That, I understand." He smiled again. He had a very warm smile. A beautiful mouth. She found herself smiling back. "My father died when I was about that age and my grandfather had to step in, too, with me and my brother. We were proper little hellions, I think, and would have driven our mother to distraction." He gave her an impish look, his dark eyes shining, and she knew at once how he must have looked as a boy, trying to evade punishment for a prank. "Thanks to old Boney, I haven't seen my grandfather in a few years, either."

"That's terrible," she said sincerely.

"No, no," he replied. "We've pushed the French out of the Peninsula. Grandfather will mightily approve."

"Oh, that was very well done," she said quickly. "But I'm sorry it had to be done at all, taking so many men like you away from their families."

"True." He shifted, turning a little more toward her. "But it's what the men in my family do. All the second sons, at any rate. We go to war."

A second son. Not the heir, the important child, but a lesser one. Gwen nodded, knowing what that felt like. Daughters were even less important than second sons. "Does the army suit you?"

The captain looked at her sharply, then his expression eased. "It does—or, did. I wanted to join the army from the time I was a boy, like my father. He was a captain of dragoons, and I never saw a finer officer. It was the only thing I ever wanted, to follow in his footsteps..."

Gwen guessed from his expression what had happened. "I'm so sorry," she said softly.

He looked away. "Thank you." A pause. "At Bergen, in the Low Countries. They wrote to my grandfather that it was a French bullet that cut him down. From that moment on, I was set on fighting the French." He smiled wryly. "Who knew we would still be fighting the French, all these years later?"

"Who indeed," Gwen murmured. "Forgive me if this is too bold, but... It must be *awful*, to be so far away and know you might never make it home, and that your whole purpose for being there is to kill other men just like you, who must also long to go home to their families."

His face grew hard. "If those Frenchmen didn't wish to be torn from their families and sent to kill other men, they ought to have stayed at home to begin with and not followed blasted Buonaparte on his campaign of destruction throughout

Europe. The Spaniards and Portuguese did not ask to be invaded, their countries looted and pillaged, their citizens savaged and killed." He caught sight of her wide eyes and cleared his throat. "I don't pretend the British army is pure and noble, but in this, we are the lesser evil."

Gwen didn't know what to say. Wordlessly she touched his gloved hand, and to her surprise he caught her hand and gripped it, hard, for just a moment before letting go. She'd meant to apologize for bringing up such thoughts, and instead felt as though he had responded with gratitude, as if it gave him comfort.

"Apologies," he muttered, before taking a deep breath and continuing in an easier tone. "Yes, war is dreadful in most ways. The army cares nothing for one's personal comfort, and often contrives the longest marches through the worst weather. One week you'll be soaking wet, with biblical downpours and swollen rivers to cross, and you'd swear you would never be completely dry again. Then the next week would be blazing hot, and you would long for even a trickling stream to dampen your handkerchief. There's rarely enough to eat—let alone anything as delicious as at home—never a comfortable place to sleep, and precious little in the way of entertainment." He heaved a mock sigh. "All in all, a distressing business."

"I'm very glad you made it home," she said in a low, heartfelt voice, not fooled by the forced cheer.

"So am I," he said with a faint smile as he stretched and shifted in his seat. "Or nearly home, at any rate." He turned his head to muffle a yawn behind one fist.

They rode in silence for a while, Gwen sobered by his words. Compared to what he had seen, losing a governess's post must seem like a trifling problem. When she glanced over, it appeared the captain had drifted off to sleep, slumped against the side of the carriage.

Covertly she studied him. He looked exhausted. She'd

already noted the dust in the creases of his coat and abruptly wondered if he'd come *straight* from Spain. He said he was hurrying home to see his grandfather, who was ill. It must be a serious illness indeed to bring a soldier home from war, through winter storms and a naval blockade.

She felt another burst of gratitude that he had offered to take her along, and resolved to be as unobtrusive as possible. She settled herself against the opposite wall and closed her own eyes.

CHAPTER 3

Gwen startled awake when Reggie grew restless in his basket, setting it rocking violently on her lap. With a gasp she sat up, clutching the basket to keep it from falling. Blinking away sleep, she peered out the window, uneasy at how thickly the snow was falling now. She must have made a sound of dismay, for the captain spoke.

"It's got worse in the last half hour. Until then we were making good time."

Gwen stifled a yawn, giving her head a brisk shake. She hadn't meant to fall asleep. "Shall we be able to make it to Blackthorpe, do you think?"

He sighed as he stretched his booted feet forward. "I hope so."

Gwen nodded and turned back to the window. She must have dozed for quite a while, as the sky was growing dark.

"I must apologize for how I spoke earlier," said the man beside her. "I didn't mean to be harsh."

"Oh, no," she murmured. "I don't see how anyone can speak of war without being harsh."

He gave his faint smile. "Laments about the food and

weather, mainly. It's been a while since I had the pleasure of speaking with a lady, rather than other soldiers."

She smiled back. "And it's been a while since I had the pleasure of speaking with another adult, instead of children."

He shifted his weight and looked puzzled. "How many children do you have?"

Gwen flushed. "Oh! None of my own. I'm a governess— *was* a governess," she corrected.

If he noted her awkwardness, he didn't react to it. "An admirable profession! Nearly as harrowing as the army, I'll wager."

Gwen couldn't help but laugh at that. "Nonsense! That is —I've never been in the army, but I adore children. There is something so wonderful about seeing the delight in their faces when they finally understand geometry, or realize they can have an entire conversation in French, or have produced a truly good drawing. There is nothing in the world as excited as a child who has mastered something new, and no greater source of pride, to those around them. I've been fortunate, I suppose, in having bright, curious children in my charge. My current family—" She stopped. The Bradfords were not her current family any longer. "My recent family," she said carefully, "had two boys and three girls, very good children. I shall miss them all."

Though not their parents, she thought, but did not say.

"And now you've had enough of raising someone else's children?"

Gwen smiled wryly. "The children were the best part of the bargain. I..." She paused, her throat thickening. "I asked for leave to visit my grandmother, and got the sack instead." She refused to cry again. Not only was it useless and maudlin, there was no reason to now; she was on her way and would be with Gran soon, thanks to the captain. "On the bright side, I can now spend all of Christmas with Gran and not have to hurry back."

"An important benefit which must not be overlooked," he agreed. Gwen was grateful he followed her lead in not dwelling on the part about getting sacked, even though she thought she'd seen his eyes flash at the word. Like him, she preferred to keep their conversation more cheerful and less harsh. "Have you traveled far already?"

"From Salisbury."

"Salisbury! That's at least two days' journey."

Hence her penniless state. Gwen nodded. "Exactly so. A very long, trying two days."

He nodded. "It's a very long, trying way from Salisbury."

She was startled into a laugh. "A very long way! When you've come from Spain, and a war, and endured many dangers along the way here. Salisbury doesn't seem so far, in comparison."

"Ah, but I was alone, and responsible only for myself." He tipped his head toward the basket, which was still rocking back and forth as Reginald circled restlessly.

"I stole him," she blurted out, and then clapped a hand over her mouth, to no avail. She began to laugh, and when the captain joined in, she couldn't stop. "He was in my employer's stable," she finally calmed down enough to explain. "There were rather a lot of cats, and the head groom was threatening to drown some of them because they were frightening the horses. This one is very friendly and I couldn't bear the thought that they might grab *him* to drown, because he would be easy to catch, so I took him with me."

"They owed you," he said firmly. "Giving someone the sack, right before Christmas!"

"Without paying my last quarter's wages, either." She tipped up the lid and slipped one hand into the basket, which Reggie promptly butted his head against, purring loudly as she scratched under his chin. "Reggie was fair compensation, though."

"Reggie?"

She blushed. "Sir Reginald Arthur Louis, Lord High Mouser."

The captain's brows went up. "I'd no idea I was inviting such grand company to share this chariot."

Reggie seemed to take that as invitation. He leapt up and out of the basket, landing on the captain's knee, causing a startled exclamation from the man. Gwen gasped, and got tangled up in the blanket as she tried to grab her cat. Reggie dodged, jumping to the front apron of the carriage, where he must have caught a blast of cold air. His ears flattened on his head, and he jumped down and tried to find his way under the blanket around Gwen's feet. When that didn't work, he wound around the captain's boots, yowling loudly.

"I'm so sorry, Reggie, stop that, come here, you wretched creature!" Gwen gabbled, trying to pursue the cat while still hampered by the carriage blanket and the basket plus its lid, which was now bouncing around the chariot. She banged her elbow on the door and exclaimed aloud as she almost fell off her seat, lunging after the cat.

"Hold!" the captain barked. Gwen froze at the command. He snared the basket in one hand and the lid in the other. He thrust the basket toward Reggie, who leapt into it at once. The captain slapped the lid on and held the whole toward Gwen.

"Th-thank you," she stammered, her heart still racing. "Naughty cat!" she whispered as she hugged the basket close.

"Are you hurt?"

She shook her head, then gingerly tilted up the basket lid. Curled into a tight ball inside, Reggie peered up at her, his eyes almost black, but then he opened his mouth and gave a wide yawn.

"That answers my next question," said Captain Fitzhugh dryly. "Mind your manners, Lord Mouser."

Gwen gave a shaky laugh as she closed the basket and buckled the strap across the lid. "He's been very patient until now! He didn't ask to be trapped in a basket for two straight days. If someone tried it on me, I would likely scratch them every chance I got."

"Perhaps he was desperately waiting for a chance at escape. Perhaps the cats overheard the head groom threatening their lives, and were in a panic how to save themselves. When you came calling with your basket, this fellow seized his opportunity to flee."

Gwen pondered it. "That's rather a lot of thinking and planning, for a cat."

"They've got to be clever creatures, haven't they, to survive? If I were a cat, living in a stable where I might be trod on by a horse at any moment, I would absolutely leap at the chance of running away in a nice warm basket with a kind young lady like you."

She gave him a wry look. "He did not leap at it. I had to lure him into the basket with scraps of bacon."

He got a knowing expression. "No wonder he leapt right in. Bacon is the way to any fellow's heart."

Gwen laughed. "Then he must be feeling very hard done by, for I haven't had any food at all for him since then."

"He doesn't appear to be weak from starvation."

"But I carried him away without even asking if he wished to come, and it's surely my duty to take care of him in compensation." Impulsively she touched his sleeve. "Thank you for allowing me to bring him along."

Captain Fitzhugh's arm tensed. His grin disappeared and he turned away from her to peer out the window. "You may wish to reserve your thanks," he said. "I do believe we're stopping."

Chapter 4

Adrian had a bad feeling.

Thankfully it wasn't the same foreboding he'd had in Spain, as he made his way to the coast and the English navy, wary of guerrillas or stray French soldiers around every turn. But the speed of the carriage, never very lively to being with, had dropped precipitously.

He'd spoken to the postilion about his desire for haste. He'd paid a premium for fresh horses at every change. And now they were proceeding at roughly the pace of a nervous bride mincing down the aisle at her wedding.

He pushed open the window, admitting a blast of swirling snow. Beside him Miss Barrett recoiled and huddled into her cloak. He leaned out and saw with unease how the snow had thickened. The horses' rumps were white with it, and the postilion wasn't much better.

In fact, as he watched, one of the horses took a stumble, his left side dipping, and the postilion reined them to a halt. He twisted in his saddle and looked back. "It's rough going," he called back. "We'll not make Blackthorpe at this rate."

Damn. "What can we make?" he called back.

The postilion raised a hand and looked from side to side. The light had gone gray and flat, and it was impossible to determine distances in the falling snow. It had been four years since he came this way, and he realized he had little idea where they were.

"Haughley," said the postilion at last. "The Black Hart."

"Very well." He knew that name, though it had been years since he ventured there. He sat back and closed the window. "We have to stop."

She inhaled anxiously. "Is the snow too deep?"

The carriage lurched back into motion, slow and halting. "I think the road is icy, or perhaps too rutted," Adrian said, trying to fight off the stab of wild frustration. Only ten miles to go, when he had covered many times that much in the last week. How dare a snowstorm thwart him now?

Miss Barrett bit her lip. "Of course we mustn't risk it. The horses do not deserve it."

He was inordinately pleased she thought of the horses rather than her own desire to reach Blackthorpe. "He says we'll stop at the Black Hart," he told her. "If we must be delayed, at least we shall be warm and well-fed."

She nodded, but looked worried.

Adrian remembered the depleted state of her purse. He started to reassure her, then decided he'd simply pay the bill when the time came. If not for him, she wouldn't be here. "It appears our acquaintance is not to be as brief as originally expected. I'm sorry for the delay."

"Oh no!" Again she touched his sleeve, lightly and briefly. Adrian noticed how she did it without thinking. Miss Barrett was an affectionate woman, it seemed. He wondered if it came of being a governess. She'd spoken fondly of the children in her care. "You've nothing to apologize for! If anything, *I* should apologize for accepting your kind invitation. It would have been far more comfortable for you to travel without me."

"But not as enjoyable," he said at once. "It's been a long time since I had the leisure to converse with someone."

"And I've told you all about how I stole a cat."

"A remarkable tale of courage and daring," he said. "I was on the edge of my seat."

She laughed. Adrian realized he really liked the sound. It had been a long time since he could sit and laugh with a pretty woman.

Actually, now that he'd had good look at her from close quarters, he was thinking she was remarkably lovely, especially when her eyes were shining at him...

Then he ruined the moment by sneezing. And again.

He recovered to see her holding out a handkerchief. He shook his head, patting his own pockets, but in the end had to accept hers. "Thank you," he said as he mopped his streaming eyes after a third sneeze.

"It's not Reggie, is it?" she asked hesitantly.

Adrian shook his head even as he sneezed again. "No, no. An old cricket injury, nothing more. It acts up from time to time in the strangest ways."

From the way she pressed her lips together, she didn't believe a word of that rubbish—but Adrian was very taken by the shape of her lips. And she didn't argue, but she did shift the cat's basket to the floor and spread the blanket over it. "Are you familiar with the Black Hart?"

"Er... Not really. I've been away a long time." He dimly remembered the time he'd been there, with some mates from university who had accompanied him home to Highvale one holiday. A blonde barmaid and a shockingly large bill were the only things he recalled with any clarity. His friend Jeremy Hanson had declared they would flirt and drink their way up the coast, and they had.

Jeremy Hanson, who had bought his commission the same year Adrian had bought his, and died in the disastrous retreat to Corunna in Spain.

Miss Barrett seemed to sense his lowering mood. She pulled aside the curtain beside her and peeked out the window. "The snow is lessening," she reported. "Perhaps we will be able to go on after all."

"Perhaps," he said, trying to shake off his thoughts. "The postilion will stop for fresh horses, and we shall be able to decide then."

"Of course." She sank back in her seat, subdued.

"Tell me about your grandmother," Adrian said, breathing shallowly to fend off another sneeze. He didn't want to think of Hanson, nor any of the other mates he'd lost. He strongly suspected they would be stuck at the Black Hart overnight, and he especially didn't want to think that his grandfather might die at Highvale while he was delayed.

Her expression softened. "She's wonderful, my Gran. She makes the best sherry biscuits I've ever tasted. Every year for my birthday she makes me a new dress, and she's quite cunning about working out which color or style I might like. One year she asked me endless questions about birds, and from all that she worked out that I would like a blue dress with green ribbons."

"Did you like it?" he asked, caught by the fond light in her eyes.

Miss Barrett burst out laughing. "*Yes!* It was exactly my taste and I wore it to rags. But how she knew that from *birds*..."

"Perhaps she knew all along what you would like, and simply spoke of birds to divert your attention," he said.

Her smile was wistful. "I daresay she did, but she refused to admit it! No, she declared she knew I wanted blue because I like the cooing of mourning doves, and she knew how to embroider the hem because I disliked crows, and the green ribbons were born, apparently, from my marveling at the flight of a flock of swallows."

"A gulp," he said.

"What?"

"A flock of swallows is called a gulp." He shrugged sheepishly as she blinked at him. "I had a tutor who was a passionate ornithologist."

"Oh my! I never knew that."

"A governess can never know too many odd facts," he said.

Her smile flickered, then returned but shakier, as if she was hiding her feelings. "Of course! Yet another good turn you've done me."

Good God. Perhaps she didn't want to be a governess. Perhaps she did, but worried about finding another post; she'd said she'd been sacked from her last one. That implied she would have no reference, which would make it more difficult to find a good post, which could be ruinous. And here he'd gone and brought it up.

He felt another twinge of regret to have upset her. Adrian leaned forward and twitched aside the curtain on his side. To his immense relief, he saw the sign of the Black Hart, with the silhouette of a black stag. "Ah, we've arrived."

She said nothing, and the carriage creaked as it turned into the yard. Adrian busied himself pulling on his gloves and leaped down the instant the vehicle stopped. He turned to see Miss Barrett, face averted, carefully folding the blanket. The basket at her feet rocked wildly.

"Do go on, sir," she said. "I just need a moment to tidy myself."

It was too dim to see her face clearly, but Adrian instantly feared she might be wiping away tears. He nodded and turned.

He told the postilion he was going ahead to reserve rooms, and asked the man to help his companion when she was ready. He strode toward the inn, swirling his cloak around him and cursing his tongue.

It *had* been a long time since he'd talked to a beautiful woman. Now it was clear why.

CHAPTER 5

Gwen took a few deep breaths as she folded the carriage blanket into a neat square. That ridiculous comment about swallows was exactly the sort of thing Gran would say, out of nowhere. It made her homesick, and anxious, and filled with gratitude to the captain for offering her space in his travel chaise. Without him, she'd still be stranded in Ipswich, hungry and nearly penniless.

She was still nearly penniless, but she was several miles nearer Gran, thanks to Captain Fitzhugh. Even if she had to spend her remaining coins here, he'd done her a tremendous favor. "Let's go, Reggie," she told the cat, who was mewing restively in his basket. "And behave yourself! I fear you are making the captain sneeze, which is very rude when he's been so kind to us."

She climbed down and noted that the horses had already been unhitched and taken away. The snow was no longer fluffy flakes but had turned to wet globs of slush. The postilion, moving stiffly, was shaking crusted snow from his coat and hat. She thanked him, and asked a passing groom if she could release Reggie in the stables. He shrugged and nodded, leading away a snow-dusted horse, so Gwen took her wriggling basket into an empty area and opened the lid.

"Behave, Sir Reginald," she whispered as he leapt out and darted behind a water pail, to glare out at her with aggrieved eyes. "I'm sorry," she added. "I'll try to bring you something tasty."

She hurried toward the inn, tucking down her chin against the icy sleet. By the time she reached the door, her face was numb and wet and she all but flung herself through the door. Then she ran right into Captain Fitzhugh's back, as he stood only a foot inside the door. He turned to steady her with a hand under her elbow.

"What's wrong?" she asked, catching sight of his grim expression.

His dark eyes swept the taproom to their left. "It appears my memory of this place is outdated."

Gwen looked. It was crowded and close, smelling of old ale and wet wool and the suffocating odor of sweat. A dingy lantern hung above their heads, the glass yellow from dirt and smoke. The smell of tallow candles pervaded the atmosphere, and more than one fellow appeared to be well into his cups. It was loud and raucous, and instinctively she moved a little closer to Captain Fitzhugh.

"The innkeeper says there are no rooms to be had," he said, stooping to put his mouth near her ear. Some men in the bar were singing what sounded like a navy ballad, very off-tune as they appeared quite drunk.

"Oh." Gwen flinched at a burst of laughter. Someone has spilled a tankard of ale, and there was some pushing and cursing.

A harried woman strode past, plates piled in her hands. She stopped short when she spotted Gwen. "Didn't say you'd got a wife with you," she accused the captain.

In an instant the captain slid his arm around Gwen's

shoulders and tugged her closer. "You didn't ask. Surely you've got something suitable for a lady. Anything at all would be greatly appreciated."

Gwen, startled, said nothing.

"I told you already, the storm caught everyone off guard," the woman retorted. She was more frazzled than angry, and she looked exhausted. "We're packed to the rafters."

A man staggered from the taproom, jostling the landlady and fumbling at his trouser buttons as he went. He seized a pot from beneath a chair, hunched over, and Gwen heard the unmistakable sound of the fellow relieving himself.

The captain gave the landlady a speaking look. "Anything at all?"

She shifted her weight. One of the plates was tilting, and a trickle of gravy ran over her wrist, making her jump. "Let me think a moment," she snapped, and ducked into the taproom.

Gwen dared peek up at the captain. His gaze was fixed on the landlady, moving through the taproom as she thumped plates down on tables. His arm was still around her, holding her snugly against him. She supposed she ought to mind that, but she really didn't. Not only was he big enough to deter any man who might bother her, he was warm and solid and he smelled far better than this inn. If she turned her head slightly to the right, she could catch a whiff of sandalwood clinging to his coat, which helped blot out the reek of sour ale and now urine.

The man behind them let out a moan. The stream had slowed to a splatter, then he thumped the pot back down and presumably did up his breeches. He brushed past them, and gave her a second, interested, look. "Evening, lovely," he slurred.

"Good evening," said the captain evenly, his arm firm around Gwen. The man glanced at him and nodded before lurching back through the taproom doorway.

"We can't stay here," said the captain under his breath.

Gwen agreed wholeheartedly with the sentiment but didn't see many alternatives. "Do you propose to sleep in the stable?" she whispered. "Is there another inn in town?"

"I doubt it."

"Then what choice is there?"

He hesitated, and the landlady bustled out of the taproom. She checked at the sight of them, then jerked her head. "This way."

She left them standing in a cramped corridor near the kitchen. It smelled somewhat better here, although the heat was oppressive. Gwen glanced up at the captain again. "What do you hope for?"

He ducked his head. "Perhaps a sympathetic vicar with some spare rooms? Or an elderly widowed lady happy to make a few shillings for the night."

She nodded, but with a sense of foreboding. It was clear the captain had more ready funds than she did, and even if he offered to pay for her, she hated to take more charity from him.

However, the uproar in the taproom had not subsided, and the thought of sitting in there all night was not appealing, especially if the captain left for a warm bed in an elderly widow's spare bedchamber.

The captain pulled out his watch, and Gwen caught a glimpse of the face. It was barely four o'clock, for all that it felt like days since they'd departed Ipswich. Of course, Gwen had risen at five in the morning to catch the mail coach, and yesterday had also been a long day of travel from Salisbury.

The landlady returned. "There's a few folk about who sometimes take in a lodger or two. I can't swear any of them have got room, but it's your best hope this side of Bury St Edmunds. I can send the lad around to inquire once he's done with his chores."

"Of course." The captain shifted, angling closer to the landlady, and Gwen, sensing what he was doing, looked away awkwardly. She heard the murmur of his voice and the clink of coins, and then the landlady was nodding and smiling. Someone shouted, and she ducked back into the kitchen.

"I did my best to chivvy her along, but it may be some time before the boy has any news," the captain said. "Shall we sit down? You must want a cup of tea."

Gwen mustered a smile. "Yes." This time, she resolved, she would pay for his tea and hers.

He hung up their cloaks and led the way into the taproom, shouldering his way through the mass of men around the long trestle table by the fire. He found a vacant seat on a bench in the corner below the windows, and glared at the two men sitting nearby until they grudgingly shifted over. Captain Fitzhugh ushered Gwen into the corner and placed himself between her and the rest of the room. He raised one hand and the landlady nodded in acknowledgement.

Gwen untied her bonnet and took it off. She'd had a bad feeling, which was confirmed as she studied it. The buckram had got wet, and the brim had begun to sag badly.

"It appears to have suffered some harm," remarked the captain.

"A serious one," she agreed, turning the poor bonnet around. "Alas. Perhaps Gran has got me a new one for a Christmas gift."

"Ah," he said in surprise. "I'd forgotten about Christmas."

"It's still over a week away," she told him. "Plenty of time."

"Not much," he said ruefully. "I shan't have gifts for anyone."

"I'm certain your presence will be more than enough gift for your family," she protested

He made a face. "A fleeting pleasure, compared to a new bonnet one might wear for a year or more!"

"Oh, no!" She twisted and gripped hand, almost fiercely. "You've been away at war. Having you return home safely after that will be better than a hundred new bonnets!"

He looked a little surprised at her outburst, but then his fingers squeezed hers. "Perhaps. I hope it will be—though a hundred bonnets is aiming far too high. I understand bonnets to be very important, and I wouldn't want to overreach."

"Better than *twenty* of the most fashionable bonnets in England," she answered fervently.

The captain laughed, and Gwen smiled, irrationally pleased by that.

The landlady wound her way through the crowded room to them and plunked down a small teapot and cup, a foaming tankard, and a glass of wine. Gwen poured her cup and clasped it close to her face, breathing in the steam greedily. She drank her tea while the captain downed his beer.

"Are you hungry?" he leaned down to ask.

She hesitated, but the soup in Ipswich had been a long time ago. She nodded. Again he signaled the landlady, and by the time Gwen had finished her pot of tea, two bowls of rabbit stew had been delivered to their table. It wasn't as good as the soup had been, but it was hot and filling. By the time she pushed back her bowl with a contented sigh, the captain had already finished his. He leaned back in the hard wooden seat, his head against the windowsill behind him, his eyes closed.

The poor man. He'd been fighting a war, sleeping in the mountains of Spain, before rushing home to see his ill grandfather. He had obviously intended to travel swiftly and comfortably, in his own travel chaise with hot bricks and a blanket. Instead he was stuck with her—and with Reggie, who made him sneeze—at this smelly, crowded inn, without a bed to sleep in. And he hadn't lost his good humor or his manners.

She eased out of her seat; he didn't stir. She collected the empty dishes from their table and carried them to the kitchen, then slipped out to the necessary. When she came back, he'd stretched out his legs under the table, but otherwise hadn't moved. As quietly as she could, Gwen shifted the table to the side, both to give him space and to shield him from other patrons. She found the landlady and asked for a blanket, which the woman handed over more willingly than expected. "I've sent young Bobby around to ask about rooms," she added. "Tell your husband."

Gwen didn't bother to correct her, since the captain hadn't done so earlier. "Thank you," she said, and went back to the captain.

He slept on, his head fallen heavily to one side. Gently Gwen rolled up the edge of the thick brown scarf he still wore and tucked it under his cheek. Aside from a frown twitching across his brow, he didn't stir. Something protective unfurled in her chest. This man had been so kind to her and offered her his protection. The least she could do in turn was make him more comfortable as he slept.

It wasn't as stifling here in this corner, where the wind found every gap around the windowpanes and made the lantern above them flicker. But the bracing air was fresh, and when Gwen draped the blanket over the captain, he sighed as if in contentment.

She resumed her seat in the corner. Tucked between him and the wall, with cool air on her face, the long day began to catch up with her as well. Despite the landlady's words, no young man had appeared in the taproom, and the landlady was still running to and fro, serving and cleaning and shaking her head at patrons. Gwen's eyelids felt heavy, and she braced her shoulder against the corner wall.

Just a few minutes' doze, she thought, and that was the last thing she remembered.

CHAPTER 6

A drian woke with his head resting on a woman's breast, his hand on her thigh.

It felt absolutely marvelous, and he inhaled, pressing his face into the soft, warm flesh. His brain couldn't quite tell him whose breast it was, but she smelled beautiful. She felt rather beautiful, too, as he moved his hand up her thigh. She stirred and her legs parted slightly, and his fingers slipped of their own accord between them. He made a low, involuntary growl of appreciation. He hadn't woken with a woman beside him in a long time, not since a brief affair with Paloma, a Spanish beauty who'd allowed his troops to shelter in the garden of her finca in Andalusia two years ago.

And he shouldn't be sleeping on a woman now. That thought bloomed in his mind as the woman in question stirred again, and abruptly he remembered who she was. He raised his head and looked at Miss Barrett just as she opened her golden hazel eyes.

She didn't frown, just gazed drowsily at him. Honey-blonde curls drooped around her cheeks, and she looked every bit as enticing as she smelled, flushed and languorous. Adrian realized she'd been asleep propped into a corner, and he'd fallen right on top of her. For a moment he didn't move, unsure how to extricate himself. Slowly he righted himself, belatedly snatching his hand from her thigh. She was thoroughly clothed, but he'd felt the intimate shape and heat of her, and his whole hand tingled with it.

He cleared his throat as she blinked wider awake. There was a blanket over him, thank God, that hid his aching cockstand. He made a fuss of fishing out his pocket watch while discreetly adjusting his breeches. Beside him, much *too close* beside him, she sat up and gave a soft gasp. From the corner of his eye, he saw that the cloth around the neckline of her dress had been dislodged, and she was trying to tuck it back into her bodice. He'd had his face pressed to the bared swells of her breasts.

Which had felt like silk against his cheek.

"It's seven o'clock," he announced without looking at her. They'd been here three hours. How long had he been sleeping on her? How had it happened? He didn't even recall closing his eyes. He couldn't forget the feel and scent of her skin. He couldn't stop wondering what it would taste like. "I wonder if the boy's had any luck."

"Oh," she said, her voice raspy. She cleared her throat. "Yes, I wonder."

"I'll, er... I'll go ask." He jumped to his feet, offered her the blanket without looking at her, and charged through the room in search of the landlady.

"Aye," she told him, when he finally located her. "I didn't like to wake the pair of you. Mr. Kittridge has a spare room he'll allow you and your wife. He's vicar at St. Mary's, but a mile up the road."

This time the words *your wife* echoed in his brain. He'd let it slide before, for Miss Barrett's protection, but now he'd had his hand between her thighs and his mouth nearly on her sweet breast. Adrian tried not to think about that, and to focus on the fact that he'd located a warm bed for the night. "Right," he said. "Excellent."

He pulled on his cloak and trudged out to the stable through the downpour of sleet, where the postilion told him in no uncertain terms that he wasn't risking his horses in this weather, not even for a short drive to the vicarage. After some argument, the stable master reluctantly agreed to lend him a horse, but only if Adrian returned the horse to his stable that night.

"I'm only agreein' on account of your lady," he warned. "'T'ain't fit for man nor beast out there, but Jeannie says she's got no rooms and the Hart can be rowdy during a storm."

"Understood." Adrian tramped back into the taproom and found Miss Barrett looking a bit flustered, but she met his gaze and smiled with relief when he told her there was a room and a horse to take them there.

"I don't think we can carry both valises and Sir Reggie," he told her.

"Nonsense! I can bundle up a few essentials and retrieve the rest and Reggie in the morning." She clasped his hand. "Thank you, Captain, for going to such lengths for me. You would be well justified in leaving me and continuing your own journey—I know you are also anxious to reach Blackthorpe—"

He waved his free hand. "I would hardly abandon you now! If not for me, you would be comfortably waiting in Ipswich, where the inn did not stink of spilled ale and piss pots."

She laughed, blushing. Adrian wondered if she knew she still held his hand. "I appreciate it more than words can say."

"I hope you still think so after our ride," he said. "We're going to get soaked."

She laughed again. "I shall hardly notice, after the rest of the day!"

For a moment he just stood there, lost in the dazzling warmth of her smile. That a woman could laugh and make light of this misadventure simply floored him. Then he went to pay the bill and discovered she had already done it, while he was in the stables. The landlady nodded briskly. "A very polite and sensible lady, that one," she said in approval. "Would that more were like her."

"I agree," he said after a moment. Miss Barrett had little money, but she'd paid for his supper and beer. After he'd fallen asleep on top of her and put his hand on her thigh.

He found her waiting, already in her cloak, by the door. She held her forlorn bonnet by the ribbons but looked determined and cheerful. He resolved that he would see her safely to her grandmother's door, as quickly as he could manage, no matter what he had to do.

"I am ready to face the elements," she told him, tugging closed her cloak and setting the bedraggled bonnet on her head.

He slapped his hat onto his head and opened the door for her. "Let's be off, then."

The wet snow had become a pelting, freezing rain, and puddles swamped the courtyard. They hurried to the stable, where the groom had a brown gelding saddled. After a quick stop at the travel chaise to retrieve what they needed overnight and a last question about the direction, Adrian swung into the saddle. The big horse shifted under him as he tested the weight. Miss Barrett waited, her bundle under one arm. He caught the wariness that crossed her face, and realized she wasn't much used to riding.

"I think you'll be better in front of me," he said. At least he could keep her from falling off, if she were in front.

"You know better than I would. I shall trust your judgement." The groom boosted her onto the saddle, and Adrian closed his arms around her. She fit very well against him, her shoulder against his. She squirmed a little, getting settled, and he thought that she felt just as enticing on top of him as she did beneath him. And when her cloak gapped open a little, he caught a glimpse of the lovely breasts he had so recently had his cheek against.

Stop thinking of that, he told himself.

"All right?" he asked.

She hugged her bundle and nodded, looking even more nervous now. "The best safety lies in healthy fear."

He paused. "Are you frightened?"

"No," she said, without looking at him. "Merely mindful of the fact that we're on a strange horse, riding into a howling storm, in the dark, following vague directions through an unfamiliar town to the home of people we do not know. I undertake such adventures every other Tuesday." She smiled a little as he laughed. "I do hope you are a captain of cavalry."

Adrian laughed again. "I was! Fear not, I've ridden through worse conditions." He pulled his cloak around them as much as possible, then rode out into the squalid night.

Icy rain lashed them like a slap, and Miss Barrett gasped, huddling closer to him. Her head tucked beneath his chin, and he caught a whiff of her scent again before the wind blew a burst of sleet into his face.

It was a little too much like Portugal, where they'd been caught in every kind of storm from blizzards to downpours. That experience came to his aid, though, as he guided the horse up the main road, turned right a half mile later, and finally saw the black shape of the church tower against the dark sky. The vicarage was just beyond it, lights glowing in the windows.

He reined in as close to the door as he could. The door

opened and a short man with a ruff of gray hair around his head peered out, lamp in hand. "Captain Fitzhugh?" he called.

"Yes." Adrian dismounted and turned to Miss Barrett. She slid gracelessly into his arms and staggered as he set her down.

"Come in, come in! I'm Mr. Kittridge, vicar of St. Mary's as you see there." He turned. "Catherine! Our guests are here."

Adrian helped Miss Barrett, who had got rather wet despite his best efforts and was shivering with cold, into the house. He paused on the doorstep and pulled the bundle of his own things from beneath his cloak. He handed them to the vicar. "Thank you, sir. See that she gets warm and dry. I must tend to the horse."

"Of course, Captain. I'll leave the latch on for you."

He mounted the horse and rode back to the Black Hart, much quicker now that he hadn't Miss Barrett in his arms. She fit just perfectly in his arms. He spent a little too much time thinking about the curve of her bottom in his lap, and then even more time thinking about how plump her breasts were when she leaned into his arm.

He was becoming far too interested in his accidental traveling companion.

He gave the horse back to the stable master and turned up his collar for the walk back to the vicarage. For the first time he didn't curse the cold rain. It might be the only thing that cooled his imagination tonight.

CHAPTER 7

Gwen felt very out of her depth as Mr. and Mrs. Kittridge and their maid fluttered around her, helping her out of her wet half-boots and cloak, bringing her hot tea and a shawl, urging on her a glass of Mr. Kittridge's own gooseberry wine. They were kind but inquisitive, and there was only so much she felt comfortable telling them.

She'd expected the captain to quickly stable the horse and return within half an hour, but the time dragged on and he didn't come. That provoked some comment from the vicar and his wife, and Gwen unfortunately had no idea what to say. She didn't know where he was, or what he was doing, and since she didn't really know *him*, she had to invent some reason why he was taking so long.

It was even more difficult when she realized they believed her to be his wife.

The landlady at the Black Hart had said it, and she'd not protested because it had felt safer. The captain had played along very readily with it as well. Too late she realized the danger of obtaining a room under that pretense: the Kittridges had only one room, and of course a husband and wife would share it.

As the evening ticked by, and the Kittridges poured more wine and asked more questions, Gwen felt her powers of invention being tested. She told them what she knew first: the captain came from north of here, near Bury St. Edmonds. She had never been there but had family in the area and was eager to see it. They were on their way there now. The captain had been in the war, yes, in Spain. He had only recently returned to England.

At that point she ran out of truth and had to create some fiction, and for some reason she embroidered it shamelessly. Gwen found herself describing how gallantly the captain had rescued her from a runaway carriage on the streets of Salisbury. Then how he had charmed her by presenting her with a kitten named Reggie. Then how he had won her heart by buying her a new bonnet when hers was ruined, but not before he had researched the latest fashion and learned her favorite colors so he could present her with a bonnet that was the most perfectly beautiful bonnet she had ever owned.

She blamed the wine. And Mrs. Kittridge's propensity for a bit of romantic gossip. By the time the little clock on the mantel tolled ten o'clock, she thought anyone would be in love with him—at least, the man she'd presented as Captain Fitzhugh.

It gave her a jolt when the man himself finally returned, soaking wet and half frozen. "I took a bit of a wrong turn," he explained as he struggled out of his sodden cloak and ice-encrusted scarf. "I mistook the road in the dark, on foot."

"Don't say you had to walk from the Hart," exclaimed Mr. Kittridge. "In this weather?"

"I promised to return the horse," he replied.

Gwen realized with a start he'd only borrowed the horse to bring her here, so she wouldn't have to walk in the freezing rain. On top of all the romantic lies she'd been telling, it was a dangerously appealing discovery. He'd better do something rude soon, or she *would* think herself in love.

The captain gave a groan of relief as his boots came off, and Mrs. Kittridge rushed to prepare another cup of tea while the vicar fetched a towel. Gwen helped him strip off his scarlet coat, which took some work with the wool as wet as it was. She noticed that it was worn, neatly darned in some places, including one long cut on the sleeve. She wondered if he'd been wounded, and hoped the coat had taken the worst of it. Mrs. Kittridge fussed with hanging the coat on a chair to dry, and Mr. Kittridge promised to work some magic on the boots.

"I've tramped this entire parish in the rain, in my thirty years here!" he declared. "I know how to treat wet boots."

Thankfully the Kittridges were soon ready to retire. They showed Gwen and the captain to a spartan but clean room at the back of the house. The maid had laid a fire, the bed was made up, and then they were alone.

Gwen, tipsy on gooseberry wine, alone with the man she'd built into a romantic hero for the Kittridges' sake, but also a bit for herself. How mortifying it would be if he knew.

"What an adventure this has become," she said lightly.

He dragged one hand over his face. "I should have protested earlier when the woman at the Black Hart presumed we were married."

"I understand why you didn't," she assured him. "I shall roll myself in a blanket on the floor."

"You will not," he exclaimed. "The bed is for you."

She shook her head. "Absolutely not. You're wet to the skin and half-frozen, *you* are sleeping in the bed."

"This floor is a far sight more comfortable than a camp bed in Spain, where I slept for the last eight months." He folded his arms—unhelpfully, as the wet linen clung to his muscled forearms, and Gwen was having a hard time looking away.

"This floor is far more appealing than the scullery maid's pallet at the Two Owls in Ipswich, or that corner booth at the Black Hart, which is where I would be sleeping if not for you."

"This floor, with this rug and this fire, is the height of luxury compared to an army tent!"

Gwen had her own arms crossed now. "And you have clearly never been a governess! I would have given my right arm for a fire *or* a rug, to say nothing of both!"

The captain stared at her, blinking. Gwen saw the twitch of his mouth and realized how absurd they were. A giggle shook her, then another, and then she clapped both hands over her mouth to muffle the gales of laughter that overtook her.

"Great God," gasped the captain, caught in his own laughter. He waved his hands in the air as if to calm them both. "They'll cast us out as lunatics."

"Rightly so," she croaked, pointing a shaky finger. "This is the m-most ordinary rug."

"And we're almost at pistols drawn over who wishes more desperately to suffer through a night on it."

Gwen had to gasp three times to get enough breath to reply. "And the fire is nearly out!"

His shoulders shuddered as he bit back more merriment. His face was flushed from laughing, and his damp hair hung in his eyes, which danced with glee. Gwen couldn't stop smiling at him. She'd met this man today, and yet he seemed incredibly familiar and dear to her.

It's the wine, she told herself, and turned toward the bed. It was a good one, nice and wide, with blankets piled on top. "We could simply share the bed," she heard herself say.

He went still, the smile frozen on his face. He, too, turned to regard the bed in question as if just becoming aware of its presence.

"It's rather a large bed," Gwen's voice went on. She certainly didn't feel in control of it. "I trust you, and I am so tired, I'll be dead to the world within minutes."

He just stared at the bed.

It was definitely the wine. She should be shocked and horrified at herself, but instead she unrolled the bundle she'd retrieved from her valise and reached for the tie of her chemisette. "Turn your back, sir."

Captain Fitzhugh spun around and faced the wall, ramrod straight, as if he were standing on parade.

Gwen took off her dress—damp to the knees and splattered with mud—and her petticoat. She stripped off her stays and pulled her nightgown on over her shift. She untied her garters and rolled off the damp stockings. Mrs. Kittridge's shawl went back around her, and she felt every bit as covered as before. "Thank you," she said, taking her dress and stockings and draping them over one of the chairs beside the hearth.

The captain didn't turn around. "If you are certain... about the bed..."

"Of course." She made herself smile, even though he wasn't looking at her. She'd said it, and she would honor her word. She'd shared a bed before—with her mother, with her cousin Mary, with various children in her care when storms frightened them at night. This was hardly different.

He cleared his throat. "Then why don't you... arrange yourself for the night."

"Oh! Of course. I've only to wash and comb my hair," she replied.

His shoulders hunched. She could see his muscles tense through the damp linen. She went to the washstand and quickly washed her face and scrubbed her teeth with a corner of the flannel. She pulled out the pins and ran the brush through her hair until it fell smoothly over her shoulders, then plaited it, only to realize she'd lost the bit of ribbon she usually tied it with. Oh well; she coiled it at her nape and slid into the bed, tucking the blankets securely around her. "Done," she whispered.

He nodded and blew out the lamp.

The fire emitted only a faint glow, and Gwen resolutely kept her face turned away, but she could hear him washing, then undressing. The soft swish of cloth as he removed his waistcoat, and the clink of his watch being deposited on the mantle. The sounds of him stripping off his stockings, and the silence as he hung them to dry on the mantle. That silence extended until she felt quite tense. What was he doing now?

Then finally the sound of breeches being pulled off. Gwen tried to keep her mind a blank but she recalled the muscled hardness of his thighs beneath hers, flexing to control the horse. A cavalry officer's thighs. He'd felt quite strong and solid all over, she thought, from his arms around her to his chest at her back. And now he was standing only a few feet away, wearing just his shirt, which was wet, he would have to take it off so it could dry—

The rustle of cloth indicated he had.

Gwen, who'd been confident she would be fast asleep as soon as her head touched a pillow, felt her every nerve buzzing with taut attention. She was twenty-five years old, not a virgin but far from experienced. She'd just lost her post, and likely any hope of finding another one as good. She should be clinging tightly to her respectability with both hands, and instead she was lying wide awake listening to a man undress and wishing fiercely that she had the right to watch. Wishing that she knew the captain, *really* knew him, and didn't have to make up romantic deeds from thin air. Wishing that the moment in the Black Hart, when she'd awoken from her doze to feel his warmth and weight against her and his breath on her skin, had been intentional, or at least meaningful, and not the result of him being so tired he couldn't sit up straight.

Wishing that the charming lover she'd created for Mrs. Kittridge's entertainment was really hers.

She didn't move a muscle as the captain moved about the room. She couldn't hear what he was doing anymore, over the clamor of her own thoughts and longings. Then the bed creaked and the mattress dipped, and the blankets rustled as he lay down beside her.

She banished her useless longings and dangerous thoughts. "Good night, Captain," she whispered.

"Good night," he said tersely.

Gwen closed her eyes and prayed for sleep.

ADRIAN LAY PERFECTLY STILL, staring at the dark ceiling, stiff and hard all over.

He was the biggest idiot on God's earth. He should have corrected that landlady immediately. He should have said Miss Barrett was his sister, or his cousin. He should have insisted they needed two rooms, or if there was only one to be had, it must be for her alone.

Instead he found himself in bed with her, after receiving a knowing smile from Mr. Kittridge with some murmured words about his bride warming him up, and he'd had to listen to her undress and brush out that shiny, silky hair and know she would be within arm's reach all night.

He couldn't survive a whole night of this. He would wait until she was asleep, then he would slide out of bed and sleep on the threadbare rug before the fire, as he'd intended. He prayed she didn't make any arousing little moans in her sleep.

He just had to wait. Adrian had a fairly accurate internal clock, and he told himself half an hour should be sufficient. She was as exhausted as he was, and she should be sleeping soundly enough by then that he could move without disturbing her. Until then, he would lie here, silent and motionless, ignoring his cock, which had stiffened to attention the moment she asked him to turn his back.

He could hear her breathing beside him.

He couldn't stop picturing her stockings draped over the arm of the chair. Nor imagining her bare legs against his. He reconsidered removing his breeches. They were wet, but perhaps wearing them would be miserable enough to keep his thoughts in line.

Beside him she shifted, just a little stretch, and his wicked mind immediately drew up an image of her sleeping naked, draped in honey-colored curls and soft linen sheets. He knew she was not naked; he'd heard her pull a nightgown over her head. He wondered what it looked like, and if it had buttons down the front that a man would have to undo as he kissed his way down her throat to her plump, tempting breasts—

A coal snapped in the fire and he flinched violently. *Half an hour*, he told himself desperately. *Half an hour.*

CHAPTER 8

G wen came awake to absolute darkness.

The bed was shaking, and her sleepy mind thought it must be Philip, the Bradfords' seven-year-old son. He was terrified of thunderstorms and would often sneak through the nursery into her room and burrow under the blankets beside her. She rolled over and put out her hand until she found his body. Gently she patted his back.

About the time she realized it couldn't be Philip, the figure was much too large to be Philip, she also realized he was crying. Almost silently, but a muffled sob now and then broke through. Instinctively Gwen scooted closer, putting her arms around him.

She knew it was the captain when he seized her hand and clutched it to his cheek, where she felt the dampness of tears. She didn't pull away, and continued patting his back, trying to provide whatever comfort she could. He must have seen terrible things in the war.

Gradually his shudders stopped, as did the weeping. She was drifting off toward sleep again when he suddenly flipped over and pulled her into his arms. She inhaled, but he just held her, as if seeking comfort. He was very warm, and Gwen realized now that she'd been cold before. She relaxed into him, draping her arm over his shoulder and absently stroking his hair.

She barely felt his lips on her temple. His hand moving on her back felt wonderful, and she leaned into it with a sigh of contentment. His indrawn breath registered, and she knew what she was doing when she consciously snuggled closer.

He touched her hair, stroking it back from her face and then combing through the length, undoing whatever remained of the plait. Gwen had always loved having her hair brushed; she tilted her head in blatant enjoyment. This time she definitely felt his mouth on her brow, and she had every chance to stop things.

She didn't want to. Not yet, maybe not at all. She'd been sacked, she had no money, and she might be about to lose her beloved gran, but she could have this.

The blankets were bunched between them, providing a barrier until she plowed one arm under it and laid her hand on the captain's chest. He responded by dragging her hard against him, his arm flexing around her waist and his hand gripping her hip. That buzz lit up her nerves again, and she realized it was arousal. She wanted him.

He pressed his lips to her jaw, his hand still in her hair. Gwen moaned at the sensation. She arched her neck again, and this time his lips touched hers, light, gentle, maddening, until she pushed into him and kissed him. His hand cupping her cheek made her shiver, and she had her arms around his neck before she knew what she was doing.

He rolled up onto his elbow, above her, and she felt his fingers at the buttons on the front of her nightdress. Heat rolled through her at the memory of waking with his head on her breast, and she gripped his shoulder, silently urging him onward.

The front of her worn nightdress parted; he seemed puzzled by the shift beneath, but a quick tug at the ribbon opened it, too, and then his mouth, hot and wet, was on her skin, tracing sizzling paths across the tops of her breasts. Gwen whimpered, arching her back in appeal.

His hand felt very big and warm when it dipped inside her nightdress and cupped one breast. His thumb rolled over her nipple and she jerked. Then he bent his head and circled the tight bud with his tongue, and she gasped aloud in pleasure.

He made love to her breasts for some time. Gwen thought she might be drowning, she could hardly breathe—it was his weight settling on top of her, his hands fondling and stroking her breasts, his mouth tasting her skin. Her hands were in his hair, and somehow her legs had got tangled around him, as if she were clinging to him for dear life.

"Guinevere," he breathed, sucking lightly at the tender skin just below her ear.

"Gwen," she gasped, turning her head to let him do it again.

His hand stroked down her side, flattening the rucked-up cloth of her nightdress. He wore a shirt, but it seemed to be twisted around his waist. He caught her hip and pulled her up into him, and she felt his erection against her bare thigh.

The feel of his naked skin against hers made her feverish. She moved without thinking, rubbing against him, and he exhaled sharply. He shifted until his left thigh was between her legs, and then he moved his knee up until he was poised above her and her legs were open wide.

His finger brushed lightly over the curls between her legs. "Gwen," he breathed again, with a note of question.

Eyes closed, she nodded. "Yes. *Yes.*"

She thought she'd break at the first delicate stroke. All her nerves seemed to pull tight, and the second stroke sent a pulse through them that made her flinch. "Yes," she choked again, as he paused, and then she couldn't speak again as he teased and stroked and even pinched until she was out of her mind, gasping and pleading for more.

His fingers were inside her, his mouth was on her breast. Climax began to build inside her belly and she strained toward him. His erection, thick and hard against her thigh, slipped between her legs and she unthinkingly ground against him.

"Gwen," he gasped. His shoulders were shaking.

She was coming, her body giving way to the pleasure he had wrought. He knew it, too, his wicked fingers inside her stroking something that seemed to make stars burst behind her eyelids. "Yes," she wept. "Please. *Please*." She tilted her hips toward him and flung back her head.

He waited until the first contraction seized her, then his hand was gone, and he spread her legs wide and moved between them, driving hard into her. Gwen grabbed his arse and bucked her hips, overwhelmed at the connection and wanting more. "Christ," he gasped at her ear, and then he was moving, matching the tempo of the glorious climax rippling through her until she was limp, and he wrenched away with a groan as he spilled himself against her belly.

Neither moved for a long time. Gwen thought she might have gone deaf, except that she could hear his ragged breathing. She groped for his hand and was reassured when his fingers laced through hers and he squeezed. She turned her head, not knowing what she would say, and his mouth covered hers. His kiss was tender, and Gwen felt a warm glow suffuse her entire body. She rolled toward him and kissed him back.

Several minutes later he sat up and rose from the bed. He gave a muffled curse as he moved about the dark room, and then he was back with a wet cloth. "'Tis cold," he whispered. "Sorry."

Gwen blushed as he gingerly wiped her belly. The cloth *was* cold, a sharp slap of reality after the dream-like lovemaking, and she began to feel awkward. She tugged her nightdress back into place as the captain moved away again. She supposed he was cleaning up himself, or perhaps buying time to think what to say. Even though he'd been an active participant, it didn't mean he would view this the same way she did. She knew all too well that the same man who seduced a virtuous girl would turn around and condemn her as loose, as soon as she gave in to him. Or perhaps he would fear that she would demand things of him and was already withdrawing.

But the captain didn't say anything, and a few minutes later he slipped back into the bed. Gwen lay frozen on her side of the bed, barely breathing, until his hand closed around hers, comforting and strong. She squeezed hard back, inordinately happy. He pulled her to him and wrapped his arm around her as if he would never let go.

Gwen melted into him. *Don't think of tomorrow*, she told herself. *Take this for what it is--only tonight.* And finally she succumbed to the warmth of a deep, sated sleep.

ADRIAN WOKE EARLY, thinking himself still sleeping in a narrow camp bed. His foot was half frozen, sticking out from under the blankets, and he felt in danger of falling off the bed.

It took a moment to realize that he was on the edge of the mattress because Gwen was pressed up against his back. An unconscious smile curved his lips as he remembered the feel of her in his arms, beneath him, around him, and the needy way she whispered *Please*.

His smile vanished as he realized what he'd done. He'd made love to the girl. He'd woken from a nightmare about a disastrous scouting expedition in Spain to find her rubbing his back soothingly, almost lovingly, and he'd clung to her as a shipwrecked man might seize a raft—and then proceeded to climb on top of her like the selfish scoundrel he apparently was.

Even worse, he wanted to do it again. He had a raging erection that twitched when Gwen sighed in her sleep and stretched her legs. Adrian broke out in a light sweat as her bare foot brushed his calf. He distinctly remembered gliding his hand down her bare leg and hooking it around his waist, right before he rode her until he almost lost consciousness. And if he turned over, he would kiss her awake, and feel her move against him, and it might well happen again.

He knew what he ought to do, the honorable thing to do. It even was rather appealing, as he truly liked the lady. She was clever, and witty, and she didn't go to pieces easily. She had a streak of artless affection that warmed his lonely soul. She cared for her grandmother and she was fond of children, a savior of cats, polite to harried innkeepers, and generous with her coin even when she had few. He liked being with her. He liked pleasing her. He wanted to know her better.

But even if he was enamored with the idea, she deserved more of a choice. She'd been under a large amount of strain, from her telling, and perhaps she'd welcomed his reckless advances as a purely physical release, or even out of obligation because he'd offered to bring her to Blackthorpe.

That thought made his stomach turn, and he slid stealthily out of bed. It was dawn, but he could see her now. Her hair, wild loose waves that spread over his pillow, looked darker in the pearly light, and her face was even more lovely than he remembered. She was beautiful, he thought wistfully, and eased the blankets over her shoulders.

And he owed her a safe trip home. That was what he'd promised her, not ruination. Not only that, he needed to get home. It was shameful how little he'd thought of his family, anxiously awaiting him, while he was enchanted by Guinevere Barrett's charm. Home was where his mind should be.

Resolve firming, he dressed in his mostly dry clothes, collected his things, and quietly let himself out of the room.

CHAPTER 9

Gwen awoke feeling warm and blissfully relaxed. She stretched out, savoring the comfort of the whole wide bed.

Her eyes flew open. She was alone in that bed, and sprawled across the middle of it, not lying decorously on her side of the mattress. She sat up in alarm even as she recognized that the captain was gone. His clothing was no longer on the chair, and the room was quiet.

She sank back down, oddly bereft. Of course she hadn't expected to wake up with him smiling down at her, ready to offer a morning kiss and perhaps even more. She blushed at the memory of his mouth on her body, and then blushed even harder to think of doing that in the light of day—she ought to be ashamed for wanting him to make love to her again. The last thing he'd said to her had been *sorry*.

What's done is done, she told herself, and threw back the blankets. It was frigidly cold in the room, which she welcomed, and she hurried into her dirty dress as quickly as she could. After tidying the room, she brushed her hair and pinned it up, then folded up her nightgown and brush before opening the door.

The maid directed her to the kitchen, where Mrs. Kittridge herself was making breakfast. "There you are, dear," she said with a smile. "Sleep well?"

Gwen blushed. "Yes, thank you. Is the captain...?"

The vicar's wife waved one hand. "Up at dawn he was, shaving himself here in the kitchen with cold water! He told Mr. Kittridge he had to go to the Black Hart and see about a carriage. The two of them set off some time ago. Now, sit down and have some porridge, a nice hot breakfast for this cold day."

Gwen sat down and ate. She had just finished her bowl of hot porridge with dried apricots when a jingle of bells sounded outside. Mrs. Kittridge raised her brows and hurried to the front door. Gwen followed close behind, and had to shade her eyes.

The rain had turned back into snow at some point, and everything in sight was covered by a brilliant blanket of glittering white. The bells heralded a small sleigh, pulled by a pair of gray horses. Mr. Kittridge waved at them from the seat, and when the captain stopped the horses in front of the house, he touched his fingers to his hat in salute.

"A fine day for a drive, isn't is, Mrs. Fitzhugh?" crowed the vicar, climbing out of the sleigh. Gwen started as she realized he was speaking to her. "I hope Catherine fed you, for the captain tells me he's anxious to be on the way."

"Of course I did, Jasper," scolded his wife. She was already holding Gwen's cloak. "Here, dear, you'll want to be off as quickly as possible, for the horses."

"Yes," said Gwen, wrapping it around her. Her bonnet, left to dry by the fire, was stiff and deformed, but she didn't have another one, so put it on. The sky blazed a brilliant, cloudless blue, and the air was sharp with cold. "Thank you, Mrs. Kittridge, for everything—"

"Of course, my dear. It was our pleasure." The woman patted her hand. The vicar was waiting to help her into the carriage. Gwen tucked her small bundle down beside her and spread the thick carriage blankets securely over herself. With a wave to the Kittridges, the captain lifted the reins and the sleigh leapt forward.

"Good morning," she said as he drove back out toward the road. The bells were louder here, and she had to raise her voice to be heard.

He grinned. The sun was blinding off the snow, and his hat was pulled low while his scarf was pulled high. All that was visible was a narrow piece of his face, eyes to mouth. "Good morning."

"I've never ridden in a sleigh," she went on, chattering nervously as she tried to think how to broach the unmentionable. Those lips had kissed her last night, all the way down to her breasts.

"The snow is only six inches deep, and it's firm. A carriage would flounder in it, but the stable master was persuaded to part with this sleigh. I was fortunate enough to be the first to ask. I daresay many a guest rising late will be disappointed, as this was the only one."

She laughed, then remembered why he had risen so early. He turned the horses into the main road, and she realized they weren't going back to the Black Hart. "Oh no," she exclaimed. "Reggie!"

"At my feet," said the captain.

Gwen lifted the blankets and peered down to see Reggie's basket next to his boots. She tugged it out and opened the lid. Reggie's orange head popped out, swiveled around to take in the snow, then lowered back into the basket. Gwen reached in to scratch his ears. "Poor Sir Reggie! I should have asked for some scraps for him."

"He's had a bit of gravy and fried egg from my breakfast at the Black Hart," said Captain Fitzhugh. "I daresay that will tide him over to Blackthorpe."

Gwen looked down, torn between being charmed that he had remembered her stolen cat, and unreasonably disconcerted that they were almost there. "We shall make it there today, then?"

"Yes, barring a washed-out bridge or other calamity."

"Surely we've had our full share of calamities already," she tried to joke, but it sounded flat.

"One hopes," he agreed.

Gwen didn't think he'd looked at her once since she got into the sleigh. Her heart sank. It was too difficult to talk; the air was bracing and her eyes ached from the glare, which the misshapen brim of her bonnet did little to block. The wind kicked up as they drove, and she had to pull a bit of her cloak over her face to protect herself from the fine mist of snow thrown up from the horses' hooves. The captain, similarly muffled, concentrated on driving. The horses seemed restive, and more than once she realized he had barely kept them on the road, or whatever passed for a road under the mantle of snow. It was impossible to tell, to Gwen's eyes, where the road even was. After an hour they stopped to change horses, but aside from a quick walk around the yard to stretch her stiff legs, they were off again.

When she spotted a sign marked Blackthorpe, she screwed up her courage. "Captain Fitzhugh," she began.

"Adrian," he said. "My name is Adrian."

She stole a peek at him. He still faced forward, eyes squinting at the horses and the road. Was she supposed to call him Adrian? Or did he merely want her to know? "I want to thank you again for taking me up yesterday. It was very generous and kind of you, and I deeply appreciate it."

"Think nothing of it." He flashed her a brief look. "I was hardly able to offer you the quick and direct journey you wanted."

"I think it's been as quick and direct as it could have been, given the storm."

He gave a nod as he turned the horses into a narrower lane. The snow lay deeper here, slowing the horses. "It's remarkable how thoroughly a storm can divert your plans."

She took a deep breath. If she was daring enough to make love to a man, she must be bold enough to speak to him about it. "And I wish to assure you that last night was—"

He coughed. "Yes. Last night."

The way he said it made Gwen's entire body flush with heat. It was the same tone he'd used when he murmured her name in question, as his hands moved over her with devastating skill, when she'd pleaded that he not stop. That he carry on and make love to her. "Yes, that," she said bravely. "I only wanted to ask for—for your discretion."

"That seems the very least you should ask for." He reined in the horses again, slowing them to a slow amble. A neat little stone cottage stood in front of them, smoke puffing from the chimney, but no other sign of habitation. He stopped the horses near the door, and finally turned to her.

To Gwen's astonishment, he reached beneath the blankets and took her hand. "It was my very great pleasure to bring you north. Never feel yourself in my debt for that, as the journey was greatly improved by your company."

She felt herself turning pink. "I think I must have been a terrible burden!"

He smiled, his faint, fleeting smile. "The very opposite." He hesitated, then opened his mouth to speak just as the cottage door creaked. "I know there is much to be said, after

last night. Miss Barrett—*Gwen*—I wish—that is, I hope—
Might I—?"

Gwen gasped, recognizing her Great-Aunt Maisie peering
out, a shawl around her shoulders. "Oh! Are we here already?"

"Larkspur Cottage, didn't you say?"

"Yes—I did—but I didn't know we were so near—" Nor
has she expected him to remember the name of the house.
What had he been about to say? Oh, heavens, she didn't need
Aunt Maisie overhearing this conversation.

Flustered, she began struggling to extricate herself from
the blanket. The captain climbed down and came around the
sleigh to lift the thick carriage blankets away and help her
down, then hand her Reggie's basket. Gwen floundered
through the snow toward Maisie, who recognized her and gave
a little cry of delight. In between her rambling explanation and
Maisie's cries to Gran that Gwen had come and Reggie's
squalling to be released, Gwen didn't notice that Captain
Fitzhugh had brought her valise from the back of the sleigh.
He set it on the doorstep beside her as Maisie flung wide the
door, calling out in reply to Gran's questions.

Setting down Reggie's basket, Gwen turned to him. There
were things she needed to say, and now that the moment was
at hand, she did not want to say good-bye to him. Even if they
met by chance in the village, it wouldn't be the same. Their
acquaintance was at an end, despite the remarkable intimacy
they'd shared. "Captain—"

"Adrian," he said again.

"Adrian." She blushed. "Please come in and have a cup of
tea," she said urgently, even though it wasn't her house or her
tea. She couldn't just let him walk away.

He smiled ruefully. "Alas, I am also rushing to see
someone."

She'd forgotten about that. "Of course," she said in

dismay. "Forgive me. I hope your grandfather recovers his health."

"As do I." He took her hand and bowed over it, touching his lips to her knuckles and lingering there a moment. "Au revoir, Guinevere Barrett."

"I don't want to say good-bye," she whispered, gripping his hand. "Please, not yet."

From inside the house came Gran's voice, weak but full of hope. Without thinking Gwen looked away from the captain, and he released her hand.

"Gwen? Is it really my dear Gwen?" Gran was coming down the stairs, slowly, clinging to the banister, but she was well enough to do it.

Gwen couldn't stop a wide smile of relief at the sight. "Yes, Gran," she called. "I'm here."

Maisie bustled back to the door, beaming. "Come in, child, come in!" Then she caught sight of Captain Fitzhugh—Adrian—and gasped. "My goodness. Sir! Come in, you are very welcome!"

He touched the brim of his hat and bowed. "Thank you, madam, but I cannot linger."

She gave him an agonized glance. He gave her his little half smile again and tipped his head toward Gran. Eyes prickling for more than one reason, Gwen ran to her grandmother and hugged her.

Maisie was still talking behind her, gushing thanks, and she heard Adrian reply as he went back to the horses. It was shocking how attuned she'd become to the tone of his voice, and now she would likely never hear it again. Gran was exclaiming over her sudden appearance, and Gwen was straining her ears, desperate for one last word from him.

"But you're crying," said Gran in concern. "What is the matter?"

Gwen dashed a hand over her burning eyes. "It was the wind. I must say, now I've got a new appreciated for a carriage with well-fitted windows, after riding in a sleigh with the wind and snow in my face."

"And a happy Christmas to you, my lord!" called Maisie behind her. She shut the door and hurried over to join them, her face wreathed in smiles. "Well! My dear, what a *marvelous* surprise! Belinda made no mention of your coming."

"I didn't know!" Gran beamed at Gwen. She was still in her bedclothes, with a thick shawl over her shoulders, but she was walking and there was good color in her face. "But we're so terribly glad you're here!"

Gwen nodded, her mind on something else. To Maisie, she said, "Did you call the captain 'my lord'?"

Maisie looked surprised. "Of course. That was Lord Westley, wasn't it?"

"No," said Gwen slowly. "It was Captain Fitzhugh. Who is Lord Westley?"

Maisie nodded. "Yes, yes, Fitzhugh. He'll be the one who went into the army. The Fitzhughs do that, have done for generations. His father died a hero, you know, back in 'Ninety-nine." She clicked her tongue sadly. "And I think there was another—his uncle? No, it was too long ago, perhaps it was a great-uncle—?"

"Who is Lord Westley?" Gwen repeated.

"The young man who just left." Maisie looked at her in bemusement. "I've never met him, but he's the image of his father. *Such* a handsome gentleman Lord Victor was! And so kind and good-hearted. It seems his son is, too, to bring our dear Gwen all the way here."

"How did you meet him, Gwen?" asked Gran with a puzzled smile. "Of course I'm very grateful to him for bringing you—"

"Who is Lord Westley?" demanded Gwen for the third time, her voice rising in agitation.

Maisie and Gran exchanged a look. "The Earl of Wroxham's grandson. His Lordship's heir."

CHAPTER 10

A drian barely registered the drive to Highvale. The sleigh felt empty without her beside him, and he even imagined his feet were cold without the cat's basket by his boots. Gwen had looked dismayed before he left her, but then she had been swept into her family's embrace, and he'd heard her exclaim in happiness as she flew to the older woman in a dressing gown.

So he'd kept his word to her. He tried not to think about how cowardly he'd been, to wait until the end to bring up the subject of last night. Everything he had wanted to say had seemed to swell in his mind until it was all a blur. He'd meant to ask if he could call on her, if they could become acquainted in more decent ways, and then he'd failed to do even that much.

Later, he told himself. Now he must focus on his own business, which promised to be far grimmer.

His mother had not minced words in her last letter; Grandfather was dying. Little else could have pried him out of the army, not when they had the French on the run. Adrian had intended to fight until Bonaparte was thoroughly beaten, to finish what his father started, but now he would have duties and responsibilities here that superseded that desire. Even had he not wanted to come, he would have been sent home by Whitehall.

"My lord." The butler greeted him with visible relief after he'd delivered the sleigh and horses to the stables with instructions on where to return them. "Madame has been expecting you."

His heart fell at the strain in his mother's face. She saw him and mustered a wavering smile. "At last, you are here! I feared the snow would delay you."

The snow, and a woman who'd made him forget that he was coming home to bury his grandfather. Adrian kissed her cheek. "I came as quickly as possible. How is he?"

"Not well." She took his hand. "He's still alert, but very weak. You must prepare yourself, dear."

He nodded. "Let me change and I will see him."

His grandfather's bedchamber already smelled of death, despite the window standing ajar. Wroxham had always been a proponent of fresh air as a cure for all ills. But not even the cold winter air could banish the scent of camphor and lavender, the sour odor of sickness.

The earl's valet, who'd let him in, quietly indicated a chair near the bed. Adrian pulled it close and sat down, reaching for his grandfather's hand. The long fingers closed around his, but weakly. Wroxham's eyes opened slightly.

"Ah," he murmured. "You came... at last."

"Yes, sir," he said with a smile. "'It took me a while to find my way out of Spain, but I am here."

"Wellington... is getting robbed," said the earl with a faint smile. "Send him my... apologies."

"He got good value while he had me, I hope."

A spark blazed in Wroxham's eyes. "Of course he did! The army owes me! They got you, they got Victor..." At this mention of his son, Adrian's father, the earl's face sagged. He sighed, sinking back into the pillows. "Ah, Victor, and Louis, and Henry... my beloved Elizabeth... even innocent little Louisa. I've buried too many. I'm glad... it's my turn."

Adrian's throat constricted. He'd been a lad of fourteen when his father was killed in the Low Countries, a young soldier when his Uncle Louis had died of a fever, and only a few years older when his brother Henry was thrown from his horse and killed. He'd only learned of his grandmother's death three months after it happened, when the army's postal delivery went awry, and his Aunt Louisa had died as a girl, long before Adrian was even born. Grandfather had indeed buried too many. "I wish you would wait a while," he said, trying to fend off grief. "I've only just returned, and not had a chance to talk to you."

"Oh?" Wroxham's smile returned, a little more like himself this time. "Brought great news, have you?"

"Yes," he heard himself say. "I met a young lady."

Wroxham's brows went up. "In Spain?"

"No. On the journey here." He paused. He shouldn't be speaking of Gwen. He should be circumspect, and call on her to see if the spark caught and burned, and most of all wait until their acquaintance could be measured in weeks rather than hours. "She's lovely, Grandfather, warm and charming and clever."

"Does this paragon have a name?"

Don't say it, he thought. His mother would quiz him mercilessly if she got wind of any of this. "Miss Guinevere Barrett."

"A lovely name." Wroxham smiled. "I give you my blessing."

He tried to retreat a little. "I've only just met her. She might not be as taken by me."

Wroxham gave a soft, wheezy laugh. "I can tell... by your expression that she is worth... trying for. Go see the girl."

Adrian pressed the limp hand gently. "Only if you will try to stay around to meet her."

"My dear boy, I will try. I will try." With painful effort, he put his other hand on top of Adrian's. "But you do not need my approval.... Always been a very... clever, sensible lad. And thank God for it. I'm sure it saved you from being shot by those infernal French!" He dissolved into a coughing fit, and Adrian lunged for the cup of weak tea on the table nearby. He caught the whiff of laudanum in it as he held the cup for his grandfather to sip.

"Call on her," said Wroxham hoarsely, when he could speak again. "I would delight in some happy news."

He shouldn't have said anything. "That seems rashly optimistic, sir. I've only known her a few days." Two, barely enough to justify calling it *days*.

Wroxham groped for his hand again, and this time his grip was surprisingly strong. "But you're drawn to her."

Adrian drew a deep breath. He was an idiot to speak of this, when he hadn't managed to speak his peace to Gwen herself. "Yes. Very much so."

"My advice is to heed it. One dance with your grandmother, and I knew. She dropped her fan at my feet, and when I looked into her eyes, I knew it was a sign from God above that she was my destiny. Forty-nine years of joy we shared."

You probably didn't seize her in the middle of the night and make love to her, after that lone dance, Adrian thought. "I've only just met her," he said again.

Wroxham feebly wagged a finger. "With some women, that's all it takes."

Adrian looked down and confessed, "She doesn't know

who I am. Westley, I mean. A simple army captain, she thinks me."

Wroxham smiled. "That... is easy to correct... Go tell her!"

When he went downstairs a quarter of an hour later, he felt both exhausted and restless. His mother was in the drawing room. She took one look at his face and opened her arms. "Oh, my dear."

His eyes burned and then he was clinging to his mother, rigid with grief as she comforted him, just as she had done when he was a boy and the earl had come to tell them his father was dead in a far-away battle. "He said he was glad it was his turn to be buried."

She sighed, stroking his hair much like Gwen had done. The thought struck him that he would want his son to have a mother like this—like Gwen—someone caring and kind and loving. "He has seen a great deal in his eighty-three years."

And what Wroxham spoke of was the half-century of joy, with his Elizabeth. Whom he'd known was the one for him after a single dance. Adrian didn't know if he really believed that, but he was sure his grandfather was correct about one thing: he needed to see Gwen. Already he felt her absence.

The butler came in with a bundle in his hands. "My lord, a groom discovered this under the blankets in the sleigh."

Adrian recognized it as he took the soft roll of cloth. These were the buttons he had undone as he kissed his way down Gwen's breasts. This was the cloth he had slid up her legs before stroking her into ecstasy. Inside was the brush whose strokes he had counted as he listened to her brush her hair; caught in the bristles were several long honey-gold strands of hair, and he knew they would smell of her.

"What is that?" asked his mother in surprise.

He stared at the thin nightgown, the small brush. No soldier could have been more economical in his choice of necessities. He himself had taken a clean shirt and stockings, his shaving kit, and a little box of tooth powder. She hadn't meant to leave it behind, but she had, because she'd been trying to talk to him. And he'd been guilty and uncertain and anxious to reach Highvale, so he'd put it off until it was too late, and her family distracted her attention.

"A sign," he said softly.

CHAPTER 11

After the emotional upheaval of the journey, life at Larkspur Cottage felt very quiet to Gwen.

Gran had indeed been very ill, so ill the doctor had sighed and said it was in God's hands. That had spurred Gran's teary letter to Gwen. Maisie, though, opined that the doctor wasn't good for much, as he tended to think every woman's illness was vague and mysterious, and she had thrown herself into caring for Gran. She was younger by almost ten years, and she had insisted that Gran would have fresh air and clean bedding every day, vast quantities of tea and soup but no heavy food, and a warm poultice on her chest every night. Gran had rolled her eyes during Maisie's tale, but with a smile.

"And you mark my words, she began to get better three days before you arrived," said Maisie to Gwen. "The very day you received her letter and decided to charge across the entire country to her side!"

"Maisie, neither of us had any idea Gwen had even read my letter," scolded Gran. "It's a coincidence."

"Nevertheless, that's the day you turned a corner, Belinda," replied Maisie firmly. "God knew you must recover in time to see her."

"If you thought pixies might have crept through your window at night to breathe good health on you, I would be grateful to the pixies," Gwen told her grandmother, and gladly let Gran embrace her again.

For the first few days it was lovely; she was overjoyed to see Gran again, and doing so well. Maisie was delighted to have someone else to bake for, and they enjoyed a feast every night, it seemed to Gwen. Reggie was welcomed into the household, and won Maisie's heart when he caught two of the mice that had been plaguing her for weeks in the kitchen.

Now that Gran was improving, though—and she declared herself vastly better, with Gwen there—there was precious little to do. Maisie and Gran lived simply, with a maid of all work and a man who came by later the day Gwen arrived to deliver coal and make a path through the snow to the well for Cora, the maid.

When Gwen finally confessed that her journey to Black-thorpe had cost her her post, there had been only a moment of shocked silence before Maisie stoutly declared that a young woman as industrious, clever, and good-natured as Gwen would surely find another post as soon as she wanted one, with Gran exclaiming in agreement.

Gwen didn't say that she wasn't so certain. She'd felt righteously upset that Sir Edmund had been so callous and rude, and she didn't regret choosing Gran over the Bradfords. But it meant she had no reference from them, which would make things harder.

She ought to look for another post, somewhere around here. Not as a governess, but perhaps in one of the shops in the village. She liked being near Gran and Maisie, and there was certainly nothing to go back to in Salisbury. The only doubt she had... was Adrian.

She had learned through a few careful questions that the Earl of Wroxham's estate, Highvale, was five miles from Larkspur Cottage. The earl was elderly, and Maisie's gossipy friends at church whispered that they'd heard he was dying. Sorrow had squeezed Gwen's heart at that, thinking of how he'd told her he was rushing home to see his grandfather. At least he'd made it in time, but it appeared that, unlike Gwen's, his journey was going to end in mourning.

So her captain would be an earl soon, and Gwen was sure she knew now why he'd been so quiet during their sleigh ride to Blackthorpe. He would be an earl, and she was an unemployed, cat-stealing governess. Of course he hadn't wanted to come in and take tea with Gran and Maisie; of course he hadn't wanted to discuss that night, even though Gwen had meant to tell him that she was equally responsible and would never expect him to do something ridiculous like marry her.

He didn't know her, and she didn't know him. She even told herself he might already be betrothed, until curiosity got the better of her and she worked it out of Maisie that the young viscount hadn't been to Blackthorpe in four years, and no one had any idea of his being engaged to marry.

Of course, Maisie unhelpfully added that he surely would be soon, now that he was home and about to succeed to the earldom. That darkened whatever emotion Gwen felt at learning he was single. It would hardly matter to her.

She felt even more awkward when she realized she'd left her nightgown and brush in the sleigh. Or perhaps they'd fallen out along the drive. She wasn't sure if she preferred that, knowing the brush—which had been a gift from her mother —would be lost forever, or the thought of Adrian's servants discovering them, with a knowing smirk about the woman who had been so low class as to leave behind her nightclothes in his lordship's sleigh.

She tried to keep her mind on Gran. On Christmas, which

was only a few days away now. Maisie was baking every day and the house smelled of mince pies and gingerbread. Neighbors came by for cups of tea and to bring small gifts; it turned out Maisie baked for a number of local families, and now they brought her bottles of elderberry wine and rolls of yarn and bundles of dried herbs in thanks. Gwen knew she should feel merry, and she was trying very hard.

That morning they had callers again, and the sitting room was filled. As delighted as Gwen was to see how dear Maisie and Gran were to their neighbors, it was a strain. Everyone gushed about her thoughtfulness in coming to visit Gran, and more than once she was invited to some event in the village, only to be told hastily, "If you're still here, that is." No one knew she didn't have a position to return to, but each kind invitation reminded Gwen quite harshly.

When Gran remarked that she missed the evergreen sprigs they'd used to decorate with, Gwen seized the chance. She excused herself and put on her cloak and Gran's bonnet, hers having been declared a hopeless case. The days after the snowstorm had been milder, and the snow was mostly gone. She let herself out, smiling at the children playing there. Their mother and grandmother were still inside, visiting with Gran. The two boys were sword-fighting with sticks while the little girl was digging in the remaining snow.

She stopped to admire the girl's work—she'd carved a design with a stick and decorated it with pebbles—and only realized someone was coming when the boys gave a shout. Someone on a horse was making their way down the lane toward the cottage.

Another guest. Gwen was glad she was going out; yesterday the butcher, wearing his Sunday clothes, had come to call with some beef filets. Gwen was sure he was sweet on Maisie, because he'd stayed and talked for over an hour, but it had been a very long hour, with the faint scent of blood in the air.

She knew she should stay and greet this guest before heading into the woods in search of greenery. The boys had dropped their sticks at the approach of the horse. Even young Mary looked up from her snow art. The rider must have gestured, for the two boys whooped and ran to meet the horse, and their excitement made Gwen smile.

Her amusement faded as she recognized the rider. He wasn't wearing his scarlet captain's coat, nor the familiar battered hat, but she knew.

It was Adrian.

CHAPTER 12

Every morning when Adrian woke, he told himself he would go see Gwen that day. And every morning, something happened to prevent it.

His family had all come to Highvale. His oldest sister was married now with two small children; he'd not met either. His younger sisters alternated between tears at the impending loss of their grandfather, and eager whispers to him about the young men they'd met lately. They made him take them into Bury St. Edmunds to shop for Christmas gifts, where they passed a shop with a blue bonnet with green ribbons in the window that caught his eye, and made him wonder if Gwen would like it.

His mother seemed determined to mother him as much as she could, and Adrian remembered Gwen saying how anxious his mother must be to have him home safe and sound. It struck him that his mother had also buried too many, including her husband and oldest son. He wished he could tell Gwen that she'd been right, and also ask her how he should react. He had been a soldier for so long, he'd forgotten how to be a son.

It hit Adrian that he was the head of the family now, a sobering and abrupt realization. He'd never even been called Lord Westley before. That had been his uncle Louis, before his death eight years earlier, and then his brother Henry, until he died while Adrian was on campaign in Portugal. Now *he* was Westley, soon to be Wroxham, not only master of Highvale but responsible for his sisters' marriages and his mother's security.

His grandfather's health fluctuated, some days reviving and wanting to spend an hour instructing Adrian on some point or other about the estate, other days declining until Adrian had to talk his weeping mother out of sending for the vicar, as his grandfather rasped that he didn't want 'that damned priest' in his house until he was actually dead.

At times, it felt as though he'd left one battlefield for another.

After a morning when Mama and Gabrielle, his older sister, had broken down in tears over the funeral arrangements, Adrian had enough. He slipped out of the house and saddled his own horse, as if he were still just Captain Fitzhugh, and headed toward Larkspur Cottage. The storm had blown out to sea and left a brilliant blue sky and winter sunshine in its place. The snow and ice that had so hampered him and Gwen in their race to Blackthorpe had condensed into a mere inch of snow packed hard underfoot.

His spirits rose as he turned down the lane to the cottage. Children's voices rang out, and he caught sight of two boys sword-fighting with sticks, just as he and Henry used to do. Two other figures were outside, both female. One was a child, and the other was Gwen.

He sat up straighter without thinking. He'd missed her even more than he'd realized. And he should have been here sooner.

The two boys came running as he drew near. He swung

down and answered their breathless queries about the horse, then offered them a shilling each if they'd take care of the beast for him.

The older boy nodded knowingly. "Aye, sir, you'll want to stay a while. Hot gingerbread, they've got in there. Mrs. Maitland's a dab hand in the kitchen."

He smiled. "Is she?"

"The best gingerbread in all of Suffolk!" declared the younger boy, who was petting the horse's nose. "I wish Mam could make it so good!"

His brother cuffed him lightly. "Mam does make good gingerbread."

"Ow! She does, only Mrs. Maitland's is better!"

Adrian told them what to do and finally turned toward Gwen. She still stood by the house, though the girl had run to join her brothers. The brim of an old-fashioned bonnet concealed her expression, but Adrian's heart lifted just seeing her again.

"Good morning," he said when he stopped an arm's length from her.

She curtsied. "Good morning, Captain," she said, then hastily corrected, "my lord."

He winced at the unfamiliar title. "I wasn't trying to hide that."

"Of course not," she said. "It's nothing to be ashamed of, unlike stealing a cat."

He stifled a surprised laugh. "See, that's why I didn't tell you, an intrepid liberator of felines. I feared to appear a pasty-faced wastrel in your eyes."

"Never," she replied. "No one who buys a hungry stranger tea and soup could be a true wastrel."

Adrian paused. "What would you have thought of me, if you'd known then?"

She pondered it, rolling her lower lip between her teeth.

Adrian tried not to stare. "That you were something of a liar," she finally said. "You concealed your name, and cricket injuries do not make people sneeze, but cats sometimes do."

He affected indignation. "Did I say cricket? No, it was a war wound. How can you question that?"

Her mouth quivered. "A war wound?"

"Yes, it was a French... hedgehog," he invented, watching as she tried valiantly not to smile. "Hiding in my trunk to ambush me. I shan't regale you with the gruesome details, but suffice to say I cannot set eyes on any creature with quills without bursting into the most violent sneezing."

She choked, ducking her head. Her shoulders shook. "Cats don't have quills," she said, her voice trembling.

"And it wasn't your cat that made me sneeze," he replied with dignity. "There must have been a hedgehog in that travel chariot at one time."

She put a hand over her mouth and glanced up at him, her eyes glowing with tears of laughter. "You're a wretched liar," she managed to gasp.

"I am," he agreed. "I dislike lying, which is why I came to apologize."

Her amusement died away. She dabbed her eyes with her fingers, avoiding his gaze, then darted a look at the cottage.

"First allow me to return something of yours." He dug the small bundle of her hairbrush and nightgown from the pocket of his greatcoat and offered it.

She blushed scarlet as she realized what it was, and stuffed it into her basket. "Thank you, my lord."

My lord. Oh God, he was making a mess of this. "I'm sorry," he blurted out. "I should have come sooner, but it's all uproar at Highvale, and I've only made it through by telling myself every night that tomorrow I would come, only for some new disaster to spring up on the morrow, until finally today I snuck away from everything to come tell you... well, that I'm sorry for not coming sooner."

"I see." Head still averted, she was quiet for a long moment. "I was walking out to gather some evergreens for decoration. Would you care to walk with me?"

Relief flooded him. "I would be delighted." *Beyond measure.*

She didn't take his arm, but they walked side by side toward the woodland that hid the cottage from view of the road.

"Very well," she said as they reached the shelter of the trees. "I am sober and composed now, if you have something serious to tell me."

Adrian opened his mouth to explain, to ask forgiveness, to ask about her family, and what he said was, "I've missed you."

Gwen's eyes darted toward him, wary and doubtful.

"I have," he confessed. "Perhaps I've no right to say that, but your company made a trip that had promised to be grim and melancholy into an adventure that made me smile and laugh. You were on the same urgent purpose as I was, not knowing what you would find when you arrived, but you faced it with grace and charm and the most stubborn good humor I've ever encountered."

Now he darted a look at her, to see how this was being received. She was listening, her face pale.

"I sent you the cup of tea and soup merely to be kind, with no expectation of anything. But when you thanked me, it felt as if I'd been waiting my whole life to hear your voice. I walked out of that inn and couldn't manage three steps before I knew I was taking a wrong turn. It was as if an alarm had been raised inside my head, warning me not to walk away from you. And... I still feel that way." He took a deep breath, because she still hadn't said anything. "So I've come to apologize for taking another wrong turn, for leaving when you wished to speak to me. I felt very guilty for what happened that night—"

"Don't," she said softly.

"But neither did I wish you to be forced into something you did not want, with a perfect stranger," he went on, even though his heart had begun to throb with hope. "You asked me for discretion, and of course you have it. But if you are willing to consider more from me... I would like it very much."

GWEN'S MIND had disconnected from her body. Physically she stood poised and still, listening to Adrian confess his feelings. Mentally she was a mess, her thoughts running in wild loops and circles.

She had no idea why she'd trusted him that day in the Two Owls inn. Respectable, sensible Gwen would never have dreamed of getting into a carriage with a strange man. Now that he'd said it, though, she realized that was why: he hadn't felt like a stranger. He never had. That night in the Kittridges' spare room, he'd felt achingly familiar and dear to her.

In the cold light of day—literally—her behavior seemed mortifying. She'd tried to think why she did it, and had considered in turn the gooseberry wine, the strain and difficulty of the journey, and the fact that she'd lost her post and felt a bit mad. All those had been discarded. Deep down, she knew she'd turned into his arms and welcomed his kiss... and more... because she'd felt an instant attraction and connection to this kind, handsome gentleman with the faintly impish smile.

Even today, when she'd felt awkward and unprepared to face him, they had instantly fallen into easy conversation. French hedgehogs, indeed. Just the thought of it made her lips curve. "What have you come to offer, in the way of more?" she asked, trying to force her scrambled thoughts into order.

He cleared his throat. "I would like to call on you and your grandmother. Take you to meet my mother and sisters, who will be wild to make your acquaintance. Perhaps take you driving in a carriage, or in a sleigh if I can locate another." He hesitated. "What more would you permit me?"

More than meeting his family and introducing him to Gran. Clutching her basket, she turned to face him. "I felt it, too," she confessed. "That you were someone I wished to know. Someone I could trust, and be easy with." *Someone I could love.*

His dark eyes grew brighter. "Then may I ask a terribly great favor?"

Breath shallowing, Gwen nodded. "Yes. Kiss me."

Surprise flashed in his face, but before she could react, he stepped forward, cupped her face in his hands, and kissed her.

She went up on her toes, kissing him back. She had to grip the front of his coat for balance, until his arm went around her waist. By the time the kiss ended her bonnet had fallen off, his coat was mostly around her, and the basket had fallen into a drift of snow.

"Goodness," she gasped, flustered. "Gran will think I've walked halfway to Norfolk for greenery!"

Adrian just laughed. He still held her close, as if he couldn't bear to let go of her, and Gwen unabashedly pressed into him.

"What was the favor you meant to ask, before I begged you to kiss me?"

"I have no idea," he said, his lips brushing her temple. "It was nothing to the one you offered."

She laughed. "Will you come in and meet my grandmother and great-aunt?" she asked shyly.

"I would be delighted. I've got it on good authority that

Mrs. Maitland makes excellent gingerbread, and I'm devilishly fond of gingerbread."

"She does. She's my great-aunt." Gwen sobered. "I should have asked. How is your grandfather?"

Adrian sighed silently. She put her hand on his chest in sympathy. "Not well. But curiosity about you has revived him. He's been prodding me to come see you."

She pulled back to look at him in alarm. "You told him—!"

"That I had met a lady he would like very much," Adrian finished. "He told me to hurry back here and hope you forgave me for ever leaving."

"Oh. He's not...?" Gwen stopped, unsure. An *earl* was discussing her. "We only just met—"

"He knew my grandmother was the one for him after a single dance. Comparatively speaking, our acquaintance is long-standing. He likely thinks I've dithered too long as it is."

She gave him a sideways look. "Nonsense."

Adrian held up both hands. "Don't look at me to argue with him." He paused. "If you are willing... he asked to make your acquaintance, too." He spoke cautiously, as if asking some tremendous favor.

A favor, on behalf of an earl. From a cat-thief governess.

Gwen resolved never to mention stealing Reggie, ever again. "I would be honored," she said softly, and was rewarded with another kiss.

"Here." He stepped back and bent to retrieve her bonnet. "Is this...?"

She gave a gasp of laughter as he fell silent, regarding Gran's ancient bonnet. "It's Gran's. The sleet on the journey here, alas, inflicted a fatal injury to mine."

His face eased as he handed it back to her. "Good." He looked up with that impish twinkle in his eye that had gone right to her heart, within the first hour she'd known him.

She laughed as she tied the ribbon. Adrian grinned, and retrieved her basket, still empty of greenery. "Come with me."

He took her hand and led her out of the trees, around to the small stable where Gran and Maisie kept their pair of goats. There he bade her wait outside a moment, and he went in and spoke to the Hayden children, who had taken his horse there. Gwen stood and listened to the even rumble of Adrian's voice, and the eager replies of the two boys. After a few minutes, Mary, their little sister, ran out and stopped short when she saw Gwen.

"I'm to go ask if there's any more gingerbread," she said. "The gentleman says he's come to visit and hopes it's not all gone."

Gwen smiled, startled. "I'm sure Aunt Maisie has made enough for a regiment, but do go ask her to save some, Mary."

The girl grinned shyly. "He gave me a shilling," she whispered, showing Gwen the shiny coin. "And he gave Bobby and Sam one each, too, for watching the horse."

"How marvelous," exclaimed Gwen. "You must have all done a wonderful job."

Mary gave her a wide, gap-toothed grin, and took off toward the house again.

Adrian stepped out of the stable, a bulky package in one hand. "I brought you a gift."

Her mouth fell open. Oh no. She hadn't expected to see him again, let alone today, let alone hear him say that he'd missed her and had been waiting his whole life to meet her. She had nothing for him.

As she stood gaping, he peeled the cloth off the object in his hands and held it out to her. Topped with a white bow, it was a beautiful peach-colored box.

A hatbox.

"I saw it in Bury St. Edmunds, when I took my sisters," he

said. "It made me think of you." His faint smile flashed. "Everything made me think of you, but this especially."

Gwen set down her basket and took the box. Inside was a bonnet of deep blue silk with pale green ribbon trim and a delicate white plume. "Oh," was all she could say as irrational happiness spilled through her.

"Your bonnet was ruined, and I thought, in case your grandmother hadn't time to get you one..." He looked down. "Happy Christmas, is what I meant to say."

She looked at the bonnet, and at the man who had listened to every word she said, and then she put down the hatbox and flung herself back into his arms and kissed him. His arms closed around her and he lifted her off her feet, and for several minutes Gwen completely forgot that she was kissing the heir to an earl in plain view of Gran, Maisie, and all the visitors at Larkspur Cottage.

"You like it, I take it," he murmured, his lips brushing her temple.

Gwen smiled, kissing the side of his jaw. "You remembered my favorite colors!"

His laugh rumbled in his chest. "They weren't even my favorite thing to remember about you." He caught her hand and kissed her knuckles. "I don't want to *remember* you, darling. I want to *know* you."

You do, she thought as her heart fluttered. "I don't have anything for you..."

He squeezed her hand. "That welcome was worth more than *twenty* of the most fashionable bonnets Bury St. Edmunds has to offer." Gwen gasped with laughter. Adrian grinned. "Allow me to overcome my poor first impression with your family. I'm very keen to win their approval."

She shook her head. "Poor impression! Maisie was in a flutter, and Gran will smother you with gratitude for bringing me safely home."

Adrian made a face. "The bare minimum a gentleman could do."

She touched his coat, smoothing the lapel she had so recently crumpled. "No. It was extraordinary. And I told them so."

They walked back toward the house, her arm around his this time. She had the hatbox in her free hand, and Adrian carried her basket. There would likely be no greenery at Larkspur Cottage this year, but Gwen suspected no one would miss it now.

At the cottage door, she paused. "This is going to sound mad to everyone. *Are* we mad?"

He stopped and faced her, wearing the same faint smile he'd worn the first time she spoke to him, only a few days and yet a lifetime ago. "Of course it's mad. It was mad of me to offer a place in my cramped travel chariot to a woman I'd never met. It was even madder of you to accept. It was mad to ride through a storm to spend the night at a stranger's home, and mad to agree to share a room, and mad to take a sleigh across frozen country to get home." He extended his hand. "It's barking mad of you to allow me to call on you at all, after I left you without apologizing."

She clasped his hand. "It feels like the most sensible thing I've ever done."

His eyes warmed. "Oh, I rather like this sort of madness. I hope you never get over it. I certainly don't intend to."

I think I'm in love, Gwen thought with a startled laugh. The very thing she'd thought, that first night in the Two Owls. Adrian looked at her, faintly puzzled, and she blushed and said, "It cannot be mad to seize a chance at happiness."

"No," he agreed. "It's far too rare and precious to risk missing out on."

Gwen's heart swelled. She'd been right, that night in The

Two Owls. *I* am *in love*, she thought, and led him inside to join her family.

EPILOGUE

ONE MONTH LATER

"Where are we going?" Gwen gasped between bursts of laughter. Adrian was leading her by the hand so quickly she was out of breath, though still giddy.

"To my favorite place at Highvale." He had already led her out of the house, through the gravel paths of the garden—now cut low and sporting heaps of straw over some plants—through the arbor covered with twisting vines, and out onto the frosted grass of the lawn. It was cold, but not frigid, and the sun was brilliant in a clear pale blue sky. Given the brisk pace he'd set, Gwen was warm. "It's just ahead," he added, slowing a little as she huffed along behind him.

She peered around him as they passed a towering oak, its bare branches swaying gently above their heads, and she heard the gurgle of water. "Oh my! Is that a folly?" she exclaimed as a wide stone bridge came into view.

"Elizabeth's Whimsey, Grandfather calls it."

The folly was part of the bridge, a round little temple perched atop the stone parapet. The surrounding greenery had been cut back for winter, but as they mounted the bridge and approached the structure, Gwen realized it must be an almost idyllic spot in spring and summer. The oak tree would cast shade over it in the afternoon. The wisteria that crept up the sides of the bridge would be fragrant with purple flowers.

"It's beautiful," she managed to say as they stepped inside. It was small, a perfect hexagon with tall arched window openings all around. A low, wide wooden bench ran around the edge, lined with plump cushions, and Gwen immediately imagined reading a good book here on a summer afternoon. Brackets held long yellow draperies in the window arches, though some had been tied open. At one side was a stout stove, glowing with heat.

Adrian grinned, stepping over to one of the windows and removing his hat. "Grandmother used to come here to paint and read. Grandfather would join her after he'd been out riding the estate. She always had biscuits and cider here for me and my siblings." He paused, gazing over the stream with a bittersweet expression. "She taught me to draw here. I sketched that tree and the house more times than I could count."

Gwen looked back. Highvale sat just above them on top of the hill that the stream encircled. From here it was intimidating, the Tudor brick towers dark against the winter sky. But Lady Westley had shown her paintings of the house and grounds in summer, when the gardens were a riot of color, and it looked far more like a home.

She slipped her hand back into Adrian's. "I see why you like it," she said softly. "Thank you for showing it to me."

He put his free hand on top of hers, still gazing at the water flowing beneath them. "I also wished for a moment alone with you."

Gwen blushed. In the month since Adrian had come to Larkspur Cottage and said he wanted to know her better, they had rarely been alone. First he'd had to meet Gran and Maisy, who had looked at Gwen with wide, astonished eyes, but quickly welcomed him. Two days after Christmas, Gwen had been invited to tea at Highvale, where she'd met his mother, Lady Westley, and his three sisters: Mrs. Penhalle, who'd urged Gwen to call her Gabrielle, and Helene and Frederica. He'd ridden over to Larkspur several days a week, but Gran or Maisy always managed to be in the room during his visits. Even when he arranged to take her for a drive, he'd shown up with his sister in the carriage, too. "You don't mind, do you, dear Miss Barrett?" Helene had cried. "Westley said you were driving toward Bury St. Edmonds, and I am longing to visit the milliner's shop!"

Adrian had caught her eye behind Helene's back and cast his gaze helplessly upward, but Gwen's heart had given a thump. He was so good-natured and kind toward his sisters.

Today had been a little different. Today, Lady Westley had invited Gwen, Gran, and Aunt Maisy to Highvale for tea, and this time the Earl of Wroxham had been there. Adrian had told her his grandfather's health was very uncertain, but that he was determined to meet Gwen. The frail old gentleman hadn't looked at all well, seated in a Bath chair with a woolen rug over his lap and a shawl around his shoulders, but he'd kissed Gwen's hand and bade her sit beside him. He was a charming fellow, even if he'd had to be wheeled from the room by Adrian after only a quarter of an hour.

Freddie, Adrian's youngest sister, had whispered to Gwen that it was rare for them to see the earl at all these days. That had made her nerves twitch, even before she'd caught Gran and Maisy with their heads together, both wearing teary-eyed expressions. Gran glanced her way and gave Gwen a tiny, incredulous smile before turning away to reply to something Lady Westley had said to her.

That was when Adrian had come up behind her and laid

one hand on her shoulder, making her start almost out of her chair. "I would like to show Miss Barrett a bit of the gardens, if I may steal her away," he'd said.

His mother had instantly cried, "Of course you should! They are remarkably lovely in winter, Miss Barrett."

"They are! You *must* see them," added Frederica eagerly, while Helene was already running to ring the bell, whereupon a footman entered almost at once with Gwen's cloak and blue silk bonnet and Adrian's hat and coat, as if he'd been waiting right outside the room for the bell. Gwen shot Gran a questioning look as Adrian took her arm and led her out, but Gran had merely beamed back at her.

"I sensed as much," she said lightly, trying to stifle her nerves. "At least, I hoped it was that, rather than your family all deciding that they wanted me to leave immediately."

He smiled ruefully. "Saw right through them, did you? I faced a dreadful choice. Confide in them that I wanted a moment alone with you and suffer their assistance, or say nothing and risk an argument that we stay indoors where it was warm."

He still held her hand. Gwen squeezed his fingers. "I don't feel cold with you."

He turned to face her. How dear to her his face had become. His eyes still felt warm as he regarded her, and she still itched to stroke back the unruly waves of dark hair that refused to stay brushed back from his forehead. "We have known each other a whole month now," he said, suddenly serious.

She gave an embarrassed little laugh. "I can hardly believe it!" Never in her life had a month flown by so quickly or so happily.

He blinked. "I hope it's not alarming."

"Oh no!" She put her free hand on top of his, so that all four of their hands were clasped together. "It's been wonderful." She hesitated, then added on impulse, "In truth, I can hardly remember when I didn't know you—nor do I wish to. Meeting you in The Two Owls may have been the single greatest stroke of good fortune I've ever had in my life."

He smiled faintly. "My darling Gwen." Then he laughed and cupped her face in his hands to kiss her. Gwen pressed into him without hesitation. He'd kissed her since Christmas, but never in such privacy. Her body responded eagerly. She had spent far too much time thinking of that night they'd spent in each other's arms, pleasing each other, holding each other. All the kisses since then had only left her restless and longing for another such night.

"You're spoiling my speech," he murmured, his fingers in her hair and his lips at her ear. Her beautiful new bonnet had been dislodged and lay on the floor behind her, and Gwen hardly noticed.

Gwen arched her back, smiling dreamily. "What speech?"

"Hmm?" He lightly nipped her earlobe. "Oh. This speech." He pulled her closer, winding both his arms around her waist. "My darling Guinevere, I can't imagine my life without you. I thank God every day for prompting me to offer you a seat in my traveling chaise, and then I thank Him again that you accepted. I bless the snowstorm that kept us together, and I even think fondly of the Black Hart for being so wholly inhospitable. My family adores you, your grandmother has given me her blessing, and my grandfather—who I vow has been holding onto life solely for the privilege of meeting you— has just today told me I'm a fool if I wait another day to ask you to be my wife."

She couldn't move.

"I love you," he whispered, his cheek pressed to hers. "Please marry me."

"Oh—!" Blushing, flustered, deliriously happy, she pulled his mouth to hers. "Yes," she breathed against his lips. "Yes!"

"You will?" He grinned so widely a dimple appeared in his cheek.

"Yes!" She kissed him again, laughing. "I've been falling in love with you since the moment we met."

His eyes grew more focused, though he still smiled. "Then you won't want a long engagement?"

Her face scarlet by now, she simply shook her head.

His smile faded away. "Very good," he murmured. With one hand he reached out and untied the draperies, which fell closed. It felt as though they were cocooned together in their own private world again, and Gwen's pulse leapt. Alone with Adrian. The man she loved. Who loved her in return. Who would be her husband—soon.

"I see why this was your favorite places at Highvale," she said on impulse. "Perhaps we could... make it even more memorable. Now that we are not two strangers who have somehow always known each other, but two friends who have somehow always loved each other."

Her fiancé's eyes grew hot. "Anything you wish," he said fervently, and then he swept her into his arms and carried her to the bower of cushions.

THANK YOU FOR READING!

If you enjoyed this story, please consider leaving a review online to help other readers. Thank you!

If you would like access to special previews, giveaways, and my very latest news, join my VIP Readers list on my website. New members get a free exclusive short story as a welcome gift.

Also by Caroline Linden

Desperately Seeking Duke

The Wagers of Sin

Scandals

The Truth About the Duke

I Love the Earl

One Night in London

Blame It on Bath

The Way to a Duke's Heart

Reece Trilogy

What a Gentleman Wants

What a Rogue Desires

A Rake's Guide to Seduction

Other Novels

What a Woman Needs

Novellas and Collections

When I Met My Duchess in At the Duke's Wedding

Map of a Lady's Heart in At the Christmas Wedding

A Fashionable Affair in Dressed to Kiss

Will You Be My Wi-Fi? in At the Summer Wedding

Make My Wish Come True

Short Stories

A Kiss for Christmas

Like None Other

Written in My Heart

ABOUT THE AUTHOR

Caroline Linden was born a reader, not a writer. She earned a math degree from Harvard University and wrote computer software before turning to writing fiction. Since then the Boston Red Sox have won the World Series four times, which is not related but still worth mentioning. Her books have been translated into seventeen languages, and have won the NEC Reader's Choice Award, the Daphne du Maurier Award, and RWA's RITA Award. She lives in New England.

Visit CarolineLinden.com to join her newsletter, and get an exclusive free story just for members.